Is today your Lucky Day?

Bryant O'Shea owns and operates O'Shea's Construction & Restoration Co. by day, and he fills in at the family-owned pub to cover when his brother has a night off. Working that night, he never expected a beautiful stranger to kiss him and couldn't remember a kiss being that hot. Never thinking it might end up being his lucky day.

Macy Greene finds herself in a little bit of a bind, not to mention wearing someone else's clothes and having on too much make-up. She was working a story, asking too many questions, and now she has two huge men following her. Macy never thought in her wildest dreams that ducking into a crowded bar to give the men the slip would end up being her lucky day.

Lucky Day

By

Trish Collins

Happy Reading!

Trish Collins

By: Trish Collins

~ ~ ~ ~ ~ ~ ~ ~ ~

Lucky Series

Lucky Day - Book 1

Lucky Charm - Book 2

Lucky Break - Book 3

Lucky Rescue - Book 4

Lucky Shot - Book 5

Lucky Honeymoon - Book 6

Lucky Me - Book 7

Lucky Number - Book 8

Lucky Guy - Book 9

Lucky Couple - Book 10

Lucky Bet - Book 11

Lucky O'Shea's - Book 12

TBA

Jacobs Series

Riptides of Love

Book 1 - Parts 1 & 2

Love's Dangerous

Undercurrents

Book 2 - Parts 1 & 2

Breaking Waves

of Love

Book 3 - Parts 1 & 2

Love's Storm Surge

Book 4 - Parts 1 & 2

Impact of Love

Book 5 – Parts 1 & 2

{1}

Bryant O'Shea finished making the last of the crown molding for the Victorian house his team was renovating. When he worked on projects like this, there was no running to the home improvement store to buy what he needed. His eye for detail wouldn't allow it, but instead, Bryant matched the style of a house's original fixtures, or he researched what was popular when the house was built. He took pride in his work, and that was one of the reasons why he had clients lined up for months.

At least today, all he'd had to do was run the router, even if leaning over and guiding the machine down the long lengths of wood was rough on his back. His arms felt like noodles, but it wasn't as bad as days when he and his men did demolition. Even though Bryant had a full crew of men, he wasn't the sort of boss who stood by and watched as his men did all the work. Instead, he worked side by side with them, getting his hands dirty. It was his way of ensuring the quality of his work. His presence and involvement on the job site meant nobody cut corners. It was his name on the trucks, and his reputation at stake, each time his crew worked a job.

After spending all day at the old Victorian, Bryant had a few hours to rest before he'd have to work a shift at the pub his parents owned. Thankfully, he only had to fill in at the pub two nights a week, when his older brother Mack had off. Occasionally one of his other family members asked Bryant to cover a shift, but with eight siblings, the family could usually find someone willing to work.

When Bryant walked into the back door of the pub, he saw his sister Raylan standing over the grill cooking steaks and burgers. Raylan was little, but she was mighty. She made everything happen in the kitchen, and she ran a tight ship. Raylan ruled in here. Bryant stepped up behind her, hoping he could get her to cook him a steak.

"Hey, you think you could make me one, too?" He asked, knowing she'd do it for him because she liked him more than any of her other five brothers.

"Make you what? I have a knuckle sandwich I was going to give Paul, but you can have it instead," Raylan said without missing a beat on the grill.

Bryant laughed, "What did Paul do now?"

Paul was just two years younger than Raylan and was fourth in the O'Shea sibling line-up. Mack was oldest, at thirty, and he ran the bar. Bryant, second oldest at twenty-eight. Raylan was just twenty-six and was in charge of all the food at the bar. Paul, the object of Raylan's anger just then, was a measly twenty-four years old. Paul was a fireman and first responder. When he wasn't at the firehouse, he helped at the bar. Paul called himself a "Peacekeeper" instead of a "Bouncer," but that's what he did.

Grace was next at twenty-two. She was going to nursing school, and she did a little of everything at the bar, sometimes waitressing, other times tending bar. Then came the twins Gabriel and Patrick and they were twenty years old and attended college. The twins recruited bands as entertainment and took food orders. Ava was the youngest female in the family. At eighteen, Ava also went to school, but she helped Raylan in the kitchen a few days a week. When Ava couldn't be there, Arlene, their mother, helped. The youngest, bringing up the rear, was Tane. He was still in high school and was only sixteen. Tane worked in the kitchen as the dishwasher. All of the O'Shea children worked their way up through the ranks at the pub, until they were old enough for the next job.

Raylan turned some burgers on the grill. She repeated Bryant's question to her, "What did Paul do now? Your brother has women calling here for him nonstop, and if he thinks I'm his personal secretary, then he has another thing coming. I came in to prepare the food for tonight, and the phone hasn't stopped ringing. They all want to know if Paul's working here tonight or if he'll be at the fire station. I told them it isn't my turn to babysit and then hang up."

Bryant asked, "My brother? Why is it that when you're pissed off at him, he becomes 'my' brother instead of 'our' brother?"

"When he acts like an A-Hole, God's gift to women, then he counts as one of you."

"I'll talk to Paul and straighten him out. I'll make sure he understands this is a place of business, not his personal answering service."

"Thank you," Raylan said, "Now how do you want your steak cooked?" Bryant kissed her cheek and said into her ear, "medium-well." As he turned to walk away, she yelled after him, "Fries or baked potato?" She heard the faint answer of "fries" as he walked into the bar.

Behind the bar, Bryant checked the work schedule. The pub didn't have many employees other than family, and those who did work there had been with the O'Shea's a long time. There was Fred, a retired cop who worked the bar during the day. The old-timers loved to shoot the breeze with him, and he kept track of the checker winners and losers. Then there was Lucile, who came in just for the lunch crowd. Lucile was in her early fifties. She was a widow and had no plans to remarry. The love of her life, her husband, was one of the first responders to go into the World Trade Center.

The nightlife at the pub had an entirely different atmosphere from the day shift. The bar had two different sections. The front section had the bar down the right-side wall, with the kitchen behind it. Some tables lined the center of the room while the booths ran along the left side of the building. The day shift hardly stepped foot in the back half of the pub. The back section was set up for bands. It had a small stage and a dance floor, made up of green and gold-checkered tiles, with high round tables and stools that lined the dance floor.

It was impossible to mistake O'Shea's Irish Pub and Grill for anything other than what it was. The walls displayed a decor portraying the luck of the Irish. The most popular one was at the door. It was a big round sign that read, "May This Shamrock Bring You Luck in Your Travels," with a huge green shamrock in the middle. It had become a tradition for customers, and everyone to touch the sign as they left the bar.

As Bryant stood behind the bar, the day crew was getting ready to switch over to the night employees. On Friday and Saturday nights, the pub was busy. Mack, his eldest brother, or Grace the nursing student helped, but Mack was off that night. That was why Bryant was filling in, and he never knew the job he might have to do, he looked to see who was working that night, and who had which duties. His sister Grace was waitressing in the bar area, and Tracy was working in the band area. Tracy was just a weekend employee. She was in her mid-twenties, and she received a lot of attention from the male patrons. They loved her lengthy blonde hair and long legs, accentuated by the short skirts and high heels that she wore. She said that her short skirts were how she made her money—that tips were much better if she showed a little skin. The O'Shea's made all of their employees wear a t-shirt with the pub's logo on it, but they didn't say what size the shirt had to be. Tracy's was at least one, if not two sizes too small, and stretched thin across her impressive breasts.

4

With the girl's waitressing and the boys on the bar, Bryant was free to fill in wherever needed. Paul was also scheduled, so Bryant went to talk with him before the bar got too busy. Knowing how Paul could sometimes be, Bryant would love to leave this conversation to Mack, but with Mack off for the night, Bryant had to take care of it. Putting the schedule back under the bar, Bryant went in search of his brother.

Paul was in the back room helping that night's band set up, moving the band's heavy equipment into place while they adjusted the sound. The pub had a built-in sound system with speakers throughout the room, with the soundboard set up on a short table at the end of the dance floor. The band that would play that night was punk, one that Gabriel, one of the twins, had picked. The twins may have looked alike, but they had completely different personalities. Between the two of them, Patrick and Gabriel had a diverse taste in music. That was part of what made the pub work—customers never knew who would be playing that night. Walking to the small stage, Bryant cleared his throat to get his brother's attention.

Paul stopped moving equipment and looked at his brother. Bryant asked, "Got a minute?"

"What's up?"

After talking to Paul about the situation with the phone calls, Paul asked how he could control the women that called the pub. Bryant didn't want a confrontation, so he just told his brother that was his problem to figure out. "I just wanted to make sure you know that no one in this pub is your personal secretary," he said.

Bryant moved back to the bar. At eight-thirty people started slowly coming into the pub, within the hour the pub would be busy. The band always went on at ten, and most people wanted to get a good seat.

Macy Greene followed her instincts, and so far, they'd hadn't let her down. When she talked to one of her cop friends into letting her sneak a peek at the police reports for the six missing girls, her senses tingled. Macy knew there was something there, even though the cops had called all of the girl's runaways. She thought that there were too many similarities in the cases. After all, six under-aged girls disappearing after sneaking into different clubs couldn't be a coincidence. The police didn't think there was a connection because the disappearances had happened months apart, and in different areas of the city.

As she skimmed over the next-to-nothing files, she couldn't help feeling she was missing something. Taking out her tablet to take some notes, Macy quickly typed the girls' names, the places where they disappeared, the dates of their disappearances, and before leaving, she finally took pictures of each girl in the files. If she took her iPad when she asked questions, she could show the pictures around. She didn't have much to go on, so she decided to start with the clubs. Slipping the files back on her friend's desk, she left the station.

Macy went from one club to the next, and just as she thought, no one claimed to know anything about the missing girls. The bouncers barely glanced when she showed them the pictures on her tablet. The last club on her list was known for its easy access for underage kids. The bouncers didn't look too hard to see if the kid standing in front of them matched the picture on the driver's license—as long as you had the ID, you got in.

This time, instead of talking to the bouncer outside of the club, Macy went in. Once she made it through the door, she realized right away that she didn't fit in. Dressed in her work clothes, a nice dress, and with next-to-no make-up on, she stuck out like a sore thumb. However, she wasn't there to party. She needed to find out what happened to those girls before any more went missing.

Inside the club, Macy started asking everyone who would stop to speak to her whether they'd seen any of the girls. First was her waitress, who was only interested in Macy's drink order. When Macy showed her the pictures the waitress said, "Do you have any idea how many people come through this club? Every night is the same. I don't remember who I served last night, much less six months ago."

Macy asked the bartender, who gave her pretty much the same reaction. The bartender wanted to know why Macy was asking questions, "Are you a cop?" he asked. Macy admitted she was not a cop, and the bartender said he couldn't help her. She asked if the owner was in the building, and the bartender nodded yes. Macy asked if she could speak to him and he put one finger in the air, pointing up. He went to the phone on the back wall, covering his ear as he spoke, and then hung up. The bartender said, "Someone will be out to get you."

Not sure where she would be going, and aware of the fact that no one knew where Macy was, she couldn't help feeling a little unnerved.

Trying to shore up her nerves, Macy found the waitress she spoke to earlier. She said, "If someone comes looking for me, I want you to remember my name and that this is the last place you saw me. I'm Macy Greene, and I work for Metro newspaper." The waitress gave Macy a funny look at her statement. Then a very large man stepped up beside her. The man was dressed in a dark suit and was clean-shaven. His head sat directly on his shoulders, with no neck. Macy took a long look at the man, trying to remember everything about him, in case she would need to describe him later.

The man stood at least a foot taller than Macy's five-nine frame. Putting out his hand to guide her into a back hallway, he pressed numbers into a keypad next to the door and waited for her to go through. There was no backing out once that door behind her closed. All of her instincts were telling her that following the man was a bad idea.

She decided she would make idle chit-chat with the hulk. "Sorry I didn't catch your name," she said with as much control as she could muster.

"I didn't tell you my name," he said.

"Okay then, what's your name? I'm Julia," Macy said. Julia was a name she used when working undercover so that no one could trace her. It was also her best friends name, so it rolled off her tongue easily.

"The name's Daniel."

"Can I ask who your boss is, so I know whom I will be speaking to?" Daniel didn't answer her. So, apparently, Danny boy wasn't giving anything away. He just kept walking until they reached another set of doors. Stopping, he knocked, and stepped just inside the doorway, and announced her. "Mr. Smith, this is Julia, and she is asking about those missing girls."

When Macy stepped into the office, the man sitting behind his desk stunned her. He was young and very handsome—movie star handsome, not at all what she'd expected. Macy had pictured the club's owner as a balding, overweight, older man. Macy had to take a few seconds to catch her breath and remember why she'd come. The gorgeous man stood and stepped around his desk. That was when Macy's senses returned, and she heard the door click behind her.

He introduced himself with his outreached hand, "Hi Julia, I'm Jim Smith."

His name made Macy laugh because you couldn't come up with a more generic name. His brow rose, and Macy covered her mouth. "Sorry, it's just your name sounds so every day. I bet there are at least a few thousand people with your name in the phone book."

He smiled at her as he took her in from top to bottom, his eyes roaming slowly over her body. "Julia, please have a seat, and we can discuss what brought you here tonight." He walked back behind his desk and sat.

Macy knew she needed to proceed with caution. She didn't want this man to be able to find her once she left—or if she left. The hairs on her neck stood, but she ignored her response to this man because she had come for answers. "I just have a few questions about six girls that went missing after sneaking into your club and a few others. You must have surveillance cameras and would know if the girls left your club with someone, or..." She stopped before she could suggest that the girls never left his club at all.

"Can I first ask why you're asking questions about these girls? You don't look to be a cop or detective, so I have to ask myself, why would this woman be poking around?"

"Sorry, I didn't state right away that I'm a reporter. I'm looking into the girls' disappearances. I've looked at the police reports, but there wasn't much there."

"I'm sorry," the handsome man said, "but I really can't help you with any more information other than what I told the police. I already gave them copies of any surveillance tapes," he finished. He sat back in his chair, watching her every move.

"Could I get copies of those tapes?" she asked, already knowing the answer before he said anything.

"Sorry, but we can't release them to just anybody. You could be working for the girls' families, trying to build a case to sue us for something or another."

"As I told you, I'm a reporter. I'm not working for anyone but the paper, but I do understand. I can get my hands on the recordings on my own. Thank you for your time." Macy got up, and Jim came around the desk to her side. He shook her hand again, but this time his other hand rested on her arm. Again, the hair on Macy's neck rose. It was time to get the hell out of there.

He held her hand a little too long as he asked, "What paper did you say you were from?"

Pulling her hand free, she said, "I didn't say. Again, thanks for your time. Do I go out the same way I came in?" Jim Smith nodded, and she turned, trying not to run out of the door. Once she was back in the hall, she couldn't help looking around. She wanted to know if there was a back door, or if there were other rooms off the hallway. Just as she started to snoop around, Daniel showed up and escorted her back out into the club. Well, she thought, at least she was free to leave, but once she was back in the club she didn't feel the need to rush to leave. Macy took a table in a corner. Watching everyone from there, she looked for girls that looked underage. When it was getting late, and she had enough, she decided to leave the club. Getting up at six that morning had done her in.

Walking out of the club, Macy watched her surroundings and noticed she wasn't alone. Two men were walking some distance behind her, but she knew they were following her. Macy began looking for a place to give them the slip. She didn't want to lead them to her doorstep. On the next corner, Macy spotted a door to some pub, where she could go in then leave out the back door. The bar looked crowded enough to lose her new admirers, but once she was inside, she realized there was no back door to sneak out. A band was playing in the back room. Macy took the last booth closest to the room with the music. She pulled out her iPad. If she was going to be stuck here, she might as well get some work done. She sat facing the door, so she knew just when the two goons slipped in. Ordering coffee to keep her awake, she started writing notes on what had happened to her since leaving the police station.

{2}

Grace pulled Bryant into the kitchen, which meant she needed something but didn't want anyone overhearing her complaints. Once they were safely through the swinging doors to the kitchen, she started in.

"How am I supposed to make money, huh? This woman is taking up a whole booth, just sitting there with her tablet and drinking coffee. She needs to go to the all-night coffee shop around the corner if she wants to work and drink coffee. It would be quieter for her, and I could get some alcohol-buying customers in that booth. How am I going to pay for nursing school if I'm not making any money? Bryant, get rid of her, please, help her move along."

Bryant looked out of the swinging door to find the woman sitting in a booth alone. He spotted her right away, moving to her table, and stood waiting for her to look up from her computer. Instead of looking up to acknowledge him, the woman slid her coffee cup closer to the edge of the table for a refill. Bryant leaned down to get her attention. "Is there anything else I can get you?" he asked. The deep tone of his voice got her to look up at him.

She sat up straight and looked him over, asking, "You work here?"

He pointed to his shirt, with its O'Shea's Irish Pub and Grill logo. "I do," he said. The woman wasn't looking at his shirt but instead at something near the bar. She said, "I need your help."

"Oh, do you need me to call you a cab?" He asked sarcastically.

The woman looked at her empty coffee cup and said, annoyed, "I haven't been drinking. I've only had coffee."

"I know, but you do know this is a bar where most patrons consume alcohol, and not a coffee shop, right?"

Now she understood why he offered to call a cab—he wanted her out of the building. Macy thought, *If only she could just walk out the door*, "I do want to leave, but I have a little problem. There are two big goons at the bar, and they're following me. I don't want to lead them to my home." Bryant started to turn to look towards the bar, but Macy grabbed his arm to stop him from looking. "Don't look at them."

Now Bryant turned the other way and stooped down next to Macy, rather than facing her. He could see the entire bar area, and sure enough, there were two big guys at the bar. Not convinced that they were following the woman, though. She could be a lunatic, a beautiful lunatic, with her dark chestnut hair that hung down past her chest. Even the big, black-rimmed glasses she wore and her prim-and-proper dress couldn't hide how beautiful the woman was.

Just as he was thinking about all the things he liked about her, she leaned closer to speak into his ear. Her voice in his ear and her breath on his neck sent chills down his body. "I know you might not believe me, but if you have a back door that I could slip out, I'll get out of your hair."

"You in some kind of trouble? You're going to have to give me more than just your word that they're following you."

13

"I'm a reporter working on a story. I've asked too many questions, and now I have two admirers."

Bryant didn't want to let the woman slip out of the pub's back door, only to have them catch her in the back alley. If they were truly watching her every move, then it wouldn't take much for them to realize what she was doing.

"Wait here," Bryant said, "I have an idea." Macy watched as he walked away. Of course, she would wait there, because she wasn't going anywhere.

Although Macy did want to get out of the pub and go home, she wasn't sure what sort of plan the guy had in mind. When he first spoke, and she'd looked into his eyes, the color she saw was somewhere between blue and green—or maybe it was both. The dim lighting in the bar made it hard to tell what color hair he had. It looked brown, but then when he went to one knee beside her, she could see a reddish tint to it.

He was cute, but not as perfect as Mr. Smith was if that was his real name. Perfect men were nice to look at but never made a great mate. Macy knew that no matter how a face appealed to her, self-centered, egotistical, and narcissistic behavior was not very attractive. She went for the down-to-earth kind of guy—a man who didn't think he was better than anyone else was. The kind of guy who would help someone he didn't know—like the way this guy was helping her now. *No, you don't have time for a relationship,* she reminded herself. *You're on a story.*

About ten minutes later the guy was back with the coffee pot. As he filled her cup, he said, "I sent a friend into the ladies' room. I want you to wait until I leave your table, and then you go into the restroom. She will explain the plan to get you out of here."

Macy asked, "Wait, why can't I just go out the back door?"

14

"If they are following you then they will see you going into the kitchen. I can guarantee you that one of them will come around to catch you before you can even get out of the alley."

He took the coffee pot and walked away. Macy had to agree with the man because he had a good point. She put her computer in her bag, got up, and walked nonchalantly to the ladies' room. Inside, standing by the sink, was a woman. Macy started to get a bad feeling about this plan.

This woman had hair that was similar in color and length to Macy's, but that was where the similarities ended. The woman had her hair teased big, and Macy wore hers straight down her back. She wore a skintight black dress that was backless. The only thing the dress did manage to cover was the woman's bottom, and it didn't do a very good job of that.

The woman wore more makeup than Macy could have used in a year. She pranced towards Macy in tall stiletto heels. Macy hoped beyond all hope that the man's plan wasn't for her to trade places with this woman.

The woman introduced herself as Angela and began rattling on about how even though Macy was a button-up type, she might be able to pull off Angela's style. So that was the plan, then. Sure enough, Macy's worst nightmare was coming true. Both women went into adjoining stalls and swapped clothes. As Macy passed her conservative dress and jacket over the divider and received Angela's mini-dress in return, she wondered if there could be any other way to escape the two men at the bar. She knew there wasn't.

Surprisingly enough, Angela's dress did fit—not that it covered everything. When Macy tugged down on the back of the dress to cover her butt, the top of the cut-away back slid down, almost showing her crack. She didn't know how anyone could be comfortable wearing a dress like this. Sliding her panties down at the waist, so they didn't show, Macy asked, "How do you wear panties with this dress?"

"Oh, I don't wear any," Angela replied. Now Macy not only wanted to get home, but she knew a very long shower would be the very first thing that she did when she got there.

Angela threw her stockings over the divider and Macy almost gagged. No way would she wear them! She told Angela to keep them. Next, the shoes slid underneath the stall wall. Macy braced herself as she slipped on the high-heeled shoes. Two things Macy never shared were undergarments and shoes. Trying not to think about it, she left the stall.

Once the women were dressed, and out of their stalls, Angela pulled a big bag out of her huge purse, unzipped it, and dumped the contents on the counter. Twenty or thirty tubes of makeup rolled around the countertop. Macy grimaced—makeup was one more thing she never shared. Not wanting to look like Angela, Macy offered to do her makeup while Angela worked on teasing her hair.

Next Angela brushed her hair down flat and removed some of her makeup. Finally, she took Macy's glasses and slipped them on. Not wanting to draw attention, the women decided Macy, now dressed as Angela, would leave the bathroom first.

As she attempted to walk in the high heels and with no glasses, out of the ladies' room, Macy stumbled right into the arms of the cute guy. He whispered into her ear for her not to look at the guys at the bar, that he would keep an eye on them.

Bryant almost swallowed his tongue when she walked out. Seeing her in Angela's form-fitting black dress was eye-opening. Underneath her work suit, who knew she hid that kind of shape? Her hair no longer hung straight at her breasts, but now it was full and wild as if she just came from his bed. Even her makeup looked great.

It was more than she'd worn before, but not so much that it was harsh like Angela. The woman's makeup made her deep brown eyes striking, especially with no glasses. She was gorgeous. Her skin was flawless, and so soft Bryant wanted to touch her. He realized he was crushing on her and he didn't even know her name.

He slung his arm around her and walked toward the kitchen door, but before they could get very far, one of the big guys started walking their way. She and Angela had been in the bathroom a while, and so the guy probably wanted to make sure she hadn't escaped from a window or something.

The woman balled her fists into Bryant's shirt, pulling him down to her, and then every thought left him. Her full lips smashed into his. The kiss wasn't a soft kiss at all. She kissed him as if there wasn't a bar full of people around them. She opened her mouth and thrust her tongue against his. The second that her tongue found his, his mind went into overdrive.

Bryant's body took over. His hands began moving on their own, wrapping around her waist, feeling her smooth skin as they settled on the top of her round bottom. He pulled her into his body, hard from years of construction work, and as she wiggled to get even closer, it made him even harder. When his mind started to clear from the initial shock of the kiss, he pulled back. She let out a little-disappointed sound that made him smile.

"We need to get you out of here," he said, "and if you keep that up, I can't guarantee that I will remain a gentleman." Being a gentleman was the farthest thing from his mind. The passion she'd displayed in that kiss was something he definitely wanted to explore. He wanted to take her to a private place, where he could have her alone all night. Then he could find every passionate spot on her body. Bryant closed his eyes for a second to gather his thoughts. He knew he needed to focus his attention on getting the woman out of the pub without alerting the two big goons.

Again, he led her toward the kitchen. This time they made it through the doors without interruption. Macy released the breath she'd been holding and stepped away from the cute guy. She'd just had her tongue down his throat, and she didn't even know his name. If he asked for her name, should she tell him her real name or the one she used to conceal her identity?

"What the hell Bryant, why is Angela in my kitchen?" Raylan yelled, looking over her shoulder as she made a salad. When Raylan saw the woman in the mini-dress turn, she realized she wasn't looking at Angela at all. When Tane heard his sister yelling, he stopped loading the dishwasher to watch the commotion.

"Ray, listen, this is…" Bryant said, looking at the woman next to him. He wanted to explain the situation to his sister, but he had to stop because he didn't know the woman's name.

"Macy," she said, giving her real name.

"Yes, Macy. Well, Macy," he said her name again as if he was testing it out. "So, two big guys—."

"Goons," Macy interrupted.

"Right, anyway, they're followed her here, and she needs to slip out without drawing attention. So, I had her switch clothes with Angela."

Raylan asked, "And Angela is wearing her clothes? Wow, I need to see this. And just what will you have to do for Angela to return the favor?" Ray pointed her spatula at Bryant, "You know what she's going to want, don't you? Man, to be a fly on the wall so I could watch you try to get out of this one."

Bryant noticed Macy moving away from him, "Don't worry, Ray, I'll fix her car or something."

"It's the 'or something' I'd be worried about," Raylan said, laughing as she went back to cooking on the grill, "Nice to meet you Macy, and good luck."

Macy could see the relation between the man who'd helped her and the woman at the grill. Even with the bandana tied around Ray's hair to keep it back, a few auburn stray curls still swept along her jaw. She and the man had similar facial features. Of course, Ray was more feminine, while the cute guy was much taller and broad. *Oh yeah,* she thought, *his name is Brian. At least I don't have to call him "cute guy" anymore.*

It was when he turned his attention back to her that Macy got her first real good look at him. In the light of the kitchen, she could see his hair was brown with red highlights running through it. She still couldn't decide if his eyes were blue or green, but they held her. His body looked as if he spent some time in the gym. His biceps pulled the sleeves of his t-shirt tight, and the shirt fit snug across his chest, going all the way into his jeans—he bulged in all the right places. He didn't appear to have any body fat on him.

Stepping close, he said, "Stop looking at me like that, Macy, I told you I'm trying hard to be a gentleman, but after that kiss…" Macy watched his Adam's apple move as he swallowed. He cleared his throat, "How are you getting home?"

"I'll either take the bus or grab a cab."

Bryant didn't want her taking public transportation dressed the way she was. No way did he want guys gawking at her—he knew what went through his mind the second he saw her come out of the ladies' room. "I don't want you to have to ride the bus, or even take a cab," he said, but his concern seemed to upset her.

"Look, Brian, I move around this city all the time. I can handle getting home on my own. Don't get me wrong. I appreciate your help tonight, but…"

"It's Bryant, not Brian. Macy, have you given any thought to the dress you're wearing, and the attention you will receive riding the bus?"

She had forgotten about the dress. Macy started pulling at the hem and tried to conjure up self-confidence, but somehow, she knew he could see right through her ploy. If only she had a long coat to cover her butt, she might have felt bolder. But Angela was wearing her suit jacket, which would at least have covered Macy's open back. Of course, since the dress was backless, she'd given her bra to Angela, too. Could the night get any worse?

"I can take you home," Bryant offered. "My truck's in the alley. You need to figure out what you want to do soon before those guys out there realize you're gone. Angela isn't going to play possum for long, and once she starts working the room, they will know you slipped out on them."

Macy knew that he was right and that she didn't want them to catch her on the street waiting to catch a bus or standing on the sidewalk trying to hail a cab. If the men came looking for her, she would be right out there in the open. She didn't have much of choice—she would be safer with Bryant than she would be on her own.

"Alright, let's go," she said, "but you are not driving me all the way home. I don't need anyone knowing where I live." Macy moved towards the back door.

He agreed with her, "Whatever you say," opening the door for Macy as he guided her through the doorway. With his hand on her back, he felt the warmth coming from her skin, and now that his mind wasn't completely fried, he could smell her beautiful scent. He was still feeling aroused, and knew he wasn't taking her home just because he wanted to make sure she made it there safely—he also knew that he wasn't done with little Ms. Macy.

Bryant moved to the passenger side of his work truck. While he wasn't a complete slob, he did work out of the truck. Today there was sawdust on the seats. He swept as much of it off as he could before Macy got in. He watched as she attempted to get into the truck without her dress sliding up. He should have been a gentleman and looked away, but his eyes stayed glued to her butt.

"I don't think you need to stand there watching me like that when you know this ridiculous dress doesn't cover anything," she said. "Or was that your plan all along?"

Bryant hadn't thought the plan through beforehand, but now that she mentioned it, it was a great plan. Once they were inside the truck and he started to back out of the alley, he told Macy to get low in the seat. They didn't need anyone seeing her leave. When Macy leaned over her legs, he could see all the way down the open back of the dress to her black lace panties that were sticking out. *Oh God, I need to stop looking at her, or neither one of us will make it out of here safely,* he thought.

"Can I get up now?" Macy shifted so she could barely see through the windshield.

"Yeah, we just passed the pub." Now that he had her alone, he wanted to know just what was going on. "So, are you going to tell me why those two guys were following you? I know you said you're some kind of reporter, but what could you be working on where guys like that would be after you? Just what were they going to do if they'd caught you?"

"I'm just working on a story, asking questions. I don't think they were actually going to hurt me. I'm sure they wanted to scare me away from looking into my story. Truly, if they don't want me digging around, then that just means I must be on the right track."

"So, what's the story you're chasing? Or is it top secret?"

"I can't share the story, but apparently I do need to do a better job of concealing who I am. I give a false name when I'm asking around, and I tell them I work for different newspapers."

{3}

Bryant didn't like the idea that someone would try to track her down or hurt her in some way. He'd driven a few blocks, knowing the men wouldn't find her, but he still didn't want her walking through the city in that dress. "Have you ever had people come after you, like tonight?" He waited for her to answer, but when she didn't say anything, he said, "Macy, please let me take you home. It would allow me to sleep tonight. It's my fault you're wearing that dress, and I feel responsible for making sure you're safe."

"I don't normally let anyone know where I live until I trust them. I don't know anything about you, except that you work at an Irish pub, and you work for a construction company."

Bryant laughed because this was the city after all and this woman didn't know him from Adam. "I'm Bryant O'Shea, and I don't only work at the pub—my parents own it. This construction company truck isn't just some truck my boss lets me use—I own the company. I restore old buildings and houses to the way they once were. When my brother Mack has the night off, I work at the pub. Mack is the oldest of the O'Shea clan, and he keeps the pub running. You saw my sister Raylan in the kitchen, and my youngest brother Tane washing dishes. The waitress that served you your coffee is my sister Grace, and the guy watching the door was my brother Paul."

"Oh my God," Macy laughed. "How many O'Shea's are there? You just named five siblings."

"Actually, there are nine of us. You're missing my twin brothers, Gabriel and Patrick, and my sister Ava. If you put us all in order, there's Mack, me, Raylan, Paul, Grace, Gabriel, Patrick, Ava then Tane." He rattled the names off as if it was common to have eight siblings.

"Your poor mother," Macy sighed. "Why would anyone want so many kids?" Macy asked, shaking her head.

"Believe me when I tell you there is nothing to pity about my mother. She is one of the strongest women I know. She kept all nine of us in line, and if anything came up that she couldn't handle, my father was there as reinforcement. We're Catholic. They're old school and don't believe in birth control. All of us were born about two years apart because that's when my mother weaned us. When we asked if we would have another brother or sister, my mother would say, "God will not give you what you can't take care of," or, "Every child is a gift from God." I always wondered if she thought the same when she was in labor," he chuckled.

Bryant realized he was doing most of the talking when he wanted to know more about Macy. "So how about you, do you have any sisters or brothers?"

"No."

"No, you don't have any, or no you don't want to tell me?"

"I'm an only child," she said as she pointed out the window. "You can find somewhere to park or let me out here."

Bryant did not intend to drop her off. He was going to walk her to her door. Macy may not know it yet, but she intrigued him, and he had plans to see her again. He squeezed the truck into a parking spot,

24

putting it in park, and turned off the engine. Shifting in his seat to face her, he asked, "How far is your place from here?"

"Just a block, but I've got it from here, thanks." When he raised an eyebrow and gave her a look, she said, "I'm a big girl, and I've taken care of myself for a long time."

Bryant reached into the back seat to pull out a windbreaker. It was a work jacket. He knew it would be huge on her although it would cover her backless dress. He handed it to her.

"Thank you," she said, slipping the jacket over her shoulders, "I'll get this back to you." When he opened his door and started to get out of the truck, Macy had to stop him. She didn't want him knowing that she planned to walk two city blocks to her apartment, alone, and she didn't want him to see her try to do it in Angela's six-inch heels. "I said, I've got it," she said, but he just kept moving until he met her on the sidewalk.

"I know what you said, but as I told you, I'm going to make sure you get home safely. It's the least I can do after the way you kissed me. So, don't even try to argue with me, because it won't do any good. Unless you plan to stand here all night..." He heard her huff, and he smiled because he knew she wasn't going to fight him.

"I should have picked someone else to ask for help. Why do I always pick winners?" she asked under her breath.

"I guess today is your lucky day."

"I wouldn't call today lucky. And about that kiss—I just reacted to the goon heading our way."

Just a reaction? No, it had to be more. "Somehow, I don't buy that's all that was going on. You could have just turned your back on him, or come close, but the way you kissed me, with so much passion, it makes me wonder how other things would be." Just then, she stumbled in her heels, and he grabbed her arm, to steady her.

"You know, a gentleman wouldn't have mentioned that kiss." She released her hold on him.

"I'm only a man, Macy, and when a beautiful woman kisses me the way you did, you must know how that would affect me. It's not every day a attractive stranger grabs me by the shirt and smashes her lips to mine. As a matter of fact, it's never happened before." He looked down to attempt to see her reaction to his words, but it was a little too dark. It was already well after midnight.

"I'm sorry, I wasn't thinking. I just reacted. I promise not to do it again." Even if she didn't want him to leave her alone, she felt it was best not to encourage him. He stepped in front of her, forcing her to stop walking.

"Macy, did that kiss do nothing for you? Because it sure as hell did something for me, and I don't want you to apologize for it, or say it won't happen again." Bryant stepped closer and brought his hands to her face as he said, "I know we don't know anything about each other, but I want to change that. I believe things happen for a reason, and meeting you tonight was the best thing that's happened to me in a long time. I don't want you to be sorry for that." He leaned down to meet her raised face and softly pressed his lips to hers.

Bryant had to find out if he'd feel the same surge of electricity as when she'd kissed him in the pub. This time he felt his heart pound in his chest, and his blood rushing south—he knew there was definitely something going on between them. When her hands came up to hold his forearms, as if she didn't want him to pull away, he deepened the kiss. As he swept his tongue into her mouth, he heard her moan. She then released that same passion he'd felt during the earlier kiss. He moved one hand to wrap around her waist. She shifted closer. There was no way that he was the only one who felt the connection. He could tell that by the way she snuggled into him.

Macy wanted to stand there all night kissing him. She took everything he was giving her, though she knew she needed to pull back. Macy knew she didn't have the time to devote to him, or the effort it would take to build a new relationship—she was trying to build her career.

Making a name for herself was going to take all of her concentration. Maybe once she got her name out there as an investigative reporter and worked her way up to be the journalist she knew she could be, then she'd have time for a relationship. However, telling herself all of the reasons not to get involved wasn't helping her pull away from him. The way this man was kissing her had her wanting to crawl up his body and never let go. He slowly broke the kiss and put his forehead to hers. Breathing heavily, Macy tried to slow her heart and regain her composure.

"Macy you can't tell me you didn't feel anything, because we both know that would be a lie."

Taking a deep breath to settle her nerves, she said, "Unfortunately, it doesn't change the fact I can't go out with you. I don't have time for dating. All my energy and focus needs to be on my job right now. You see, I have nothing to offer you. My work has to come first. Maybe one day when my career takes off, then I'll have time to devote to someone."

This was not what he wanted to hear. Why would God throw this woman into his path, only to yank her away? The way he was feeling had to mean something, and he could be just as determined as she was. He wouldn't argue with her about dating now, because he wasn't done with her. He'd make sure of it.

"Let's get you home. It's late."

Macy and Bryant walked silently toward her apartment building. The only thing she knew for sure was the warmth she felt from his hand in hers, even though he probably only held her hand to ensure she didn't fall in those heels. Without her glasses, she wasn't blind, but things were a little blurry. In the dark, with the sidewalk uneven, it was difficult to walk. She wasn't used to heels that tall. When she wore heels for work, they were low, for comfort and sensibility. Macy didn't have any use for heels so high, heels like that were for women who like to draw attention to themselves—male attention. Not only was she having a hard time walking in the shoes, but they also were beginning to hurt her feet.

Just as she thought about wanting to be home, freshly showered and in her pajamas, Macy stepped on a crack in the sidewalk and went down. With the heel of her shoe stuck in the sidewalk and her body going in the opposite direction, the pain shot up Macy's ankle. Bryant tried to catch her, but she had already twisted her ankle. "Oh my God, Macy, are you okay?" Bryant knelt, slipped the shoe off her foot, and pulled it free from the sidewalk. In the dim light, he examined the already swelling joint.

Macy closed her eyes and wondered if her night could get any worse. When she opened her eyes, she realized that her barely-there dress and Bryant's jacket were both up around her waist. Trying to hold on to the little bit of dignity she had left, Macy pulled on the garments.

"Damn it's already starting to swell," Bryant said, looking up at her. He pulled off her other shoe to compare her ankles.

Bryant had his hands on her legs, running them up and down over her skin. She was in pain, yet under his touch, her body went on high alert. Once the initial shock passed, she said, "I'm fine. Just give me the damn shoes back so I can get the hell home."

"You're kidding, right? Because one, this shoe isn't going to go back on, and two, there is no way you can walk on that ankle, much less in these shoes."

"Bryant, I just want to go home. At this point, I will crawl if I have to."

At that, he slipped his fingers into the straps of the shoes, stood up, and then scooped Macy up into his arms. "Bryant, what are you doing? You can't carry me! At least let me fix this dumb dress—my butt is sticking out."

He placed her back down onto her good leg and watched her tug at the dress, and then scooped her back up into his arms. Now that he had her close, he could smell the flowery scent coming from her hair again. He couldn't help leaning in closer to fill his lungs with her smell. She held on by wrapping her arms around his neck, and he liked having her close.

"Don't worry about me carrying you, because you're light as a feather. I carry heavier loads at work all of the time."

"Loads, huh? Well, that's a great description. I'm not a heavy load, but still, I'm a load just the same. It's a good thing you don't have to carry me that far because my apartment building is coming up."

"I'm lucky that I get to hold you close. I'm not happy that you got hurt, of course, but I'm not going to complain." He smiled down at her when she looked up at him.

"We're here," she nudged her head in the direction of her door. As Bryant walked up the stairs to her doorway, Macy reached into Angela's bag to grab her key. Now that Bryant was there, maybe she could give him Angela's clothes, and then later she could get her things back. There was nothing about what she wore right now that she would ever want to keep, but she did need to get her glasses

29

back, and her messenger bag. She knew how women could be about their purses, and she was sure Angela would want her own things back too.

Macy didn't carry anything in her bag that wasn't necessary. She didn't carry a big bag of makeup like Angela, just a tube of lipstick or gloss, and of course, she kept a can of mace. Keep it simple—that was her motto. The less she had to lug around meant the more freely she could move. Besides, at the end of the day, she was tired enough from work and didn't need to add weightlifting to her day.

Bryant entered her building. As he carried Macy toward the elevators, he noticed a wall of mailboxes in the lobby. That late at night the building was quiet, so the elevator doors opened right away. As they stepped into the elevator, he thought now he not only knew where she lived, but he would also get to see her apartment. When the doors closed, he leaned over so Macy could push the button for her floor.

"You okay? You're quiet. I'm sure tonight didn't go quite the way you planned. Between the men following you, to you waring this dress, and then twisting your ankle. But I am glad that I met you, though." The doors to the elevator opened on the tenth floor, and he stepped out. "Right or left?" he asked, walking in the direction she pointed. He knew she didn't feel comfortable with him being at her apartment. He carried her down the plain hallway. Her building wasn't grand, nor was it the slums. The walls were white, and the floors had white speckled industrial linoleum squares. Nothing stood out it was clean but bland. Bryant's eye for construction told him with a little TLC the building could be a lot nicer. It was all in the details—adding some molding or even making the walls two-toned would make a big difference.

"We're here," she said, pulling him away from his thoughts of how to spruce up her building. "You can put me down now." He didn't want to let her go, but he set her down on her good leg and watched as she searched for her keys in Angela's huge bag. After a moment, he took the bag from her and began rummaging through it.

Macy asked, "Um, what are you doing?" He had to laugh at the look she gave him.

"I don't want you to fall over while you're trying to find your keys in this suitcase." He pulled a set of keys free and held them up. "Is this what you were looking for?" She snatched them from him and unlocked her door. Hopping on one foot, she tried to make her way into her apartment. He swooped in to pick her up again and flipped on the light switch by the door with his elbow and set her down on the couch.

"Where is your kitchen?" he asked as he walked through her place as if he were a guest in her home.

"Wait, why are you looking for my kitchen? I'm home safe and sound, just like you wanted. Now you can go home without any worries."

Bryant paid her no mind, turning on lights as he went deeper into the apartment. With the lights on, he easily found her kitchen and started looking for the items he needed. "Where do you keep your dish towels?"

"There's one on the stove handle. Why do you want a dishtowel?" Macy tried to turn around so she could see him, but she didn't have a direct view. Then as she heard cabinet doors opening and closing, she asked, "What are you looking for now?"

"Where do you keep your storage bags?"

Macy said, "The bags are in the closet, on the door." She was so tired and rested head on the arm of the sofa. With her ankle throbbing, she didn't think she was going to get any sleep. As she closed her eyes, she could still hear Bryant rattling around, but she just didn't care anymore.

"Okay, one more thing," his voice came closer. Without opening her eyes, Macy asked, "What now?"

"Ibuprofen, where do you keep it?"

She answered, "Bathroom, medicine cabinet, at the end of the hall." Macy had desperately wanted a shower, but now she thought she just might stay right there on the couch. Maybe if she pretended to be dead, he would leave her alone.

Her eyes flew open when she felt the cold hit her skin. Bryant had placed the dishtowel around her ankle then placed a bag of ice on it. He lifted her leg to wrap it in clear plastic, to hold the ice in place, then he handed her a glass of water.

"Sit up a bit and take the ibuprofen. It will help with the pain," he said, handing her a few tablets.

Macy began to say, "I need to take a shower, but it's just too much effort, getting in and out. I'm tired, and I might just stay right here, in this getup," she motioned her hand down her body.

Bryant's eyes went straight to her bare legs. Immediately he thought of her naked and wet body, showering. He had to get his mind off Macy in the bathroom and offer to help her—if she'd accept it. "I could help you."

"NO."

"Macy, I'll carry you in, and then you can sit and undress. Then put on a robe or something, and I'll help you in. Then put the robe back on when you finish, and I'll carry you to your room."

"No."

"Be reasonable. I promise to be a total gentleman." He watched as she put her head in her hand, taking deep breaths. Crouching in front of her, he said, "Macy, listen, I got you into this mess. If it weren't for me, you wouldn't have twisted your ankle."

{4}

Macy looked at him, and she said, "No, I got myself in this mess all on my own, starting with asking too many questions in front of the wrong people. Well, actually, it was the right people, just not in a good way. I shouldn't have tipped them off the way I did. Then I wouldn't have had to slip into your bar trying to lose those guys or switch clothes with a hoochie mama—no offense. Not to mention walking in those shoes, the ones I have no business wearing. Then I wouldn't have twisted my ankle."

"I do appreciate your help. I already made you leave your job and carry me home. I can't ask you to help me any more than I already have." Macy knew she was babbling, but that's how she got when she was past tired.

"You didn't ask for help, I volunteered," he said with a smile.

Macy thought, *Oh my God, this guy is so cute. The way he's almost sitting on her floor, and so close that if she leaned in, she could kiss him. No, you don't need to do anything else to encourage him.* Even as she scolded herself with those words in her head, she still wanted to kiss him.

"Bryant," she said his name in an almost whisper.

"Yeah," he looked into her eyes.

"I want to kiss you and I shouldn't."

Bryant asked, "Why not?" He would have liked to be kissing her too just then—and more.

Macy said, "It's not a good idea. Now help me to the bathroom, please." He smiled a little-crooked smirk and lifted her off the couch.

Bryant walked her down the hall to the bathroom. Once inside, he sat her on the side of the tub and started to leave, but she stopped him.

"Wait," she said. Bryant stopped in his tracks, hoping she would ask him to stay.

"Can you grab my robe off the back of my bedroom door?"

By the end of the night, Bryant would have been in every room of her apartment. Now that he'd seen her bedroom, not only would he be thinking about her showering, but also about her in her bed—the bed he wouldn't mind sharing with her.

As he flicked on the light, he got his first look into her personal world. Yes, he had been in the rest of the apartment, but that was nothing like being in the private space of the bedroom. She didn't have any pink frilly bedspread or lacy curtains as he'd imagined a prim and proper reporter might. Nope, her bed cover was an old-looking quilt in blues and greens. The windows had light green curtains that puddled onto the floor. Her room was neat, with no clothes lying around. A book sat on her nightstand, and a small lamp, but nothing else. It took all he had to grab just the bathrobe and walk out.

After he handed her the robe, Bryant shut the bathroom door behind him. He needed to call his brother to let him know he wouldn't be back in time to close the bar. It wouldn't be a big deal because he knew Paul could handle it on his own. As he talked to Paul, Bryant examined a bookshelf that occupied a small alcove in the living room. Macy had two pictures on the middle shelf. One looked to be from when she graduated from college. She stood between an older man and woman, obviously her parents. The other photo had her and another woman as they posed together, but it said nothing about when the photo was taken. Both women smiled as they appeared to be close—maybe a best friend. She'd said she had no siblings so that couldn't be a sister.

Bryant looked over the books. Most were on journalism, but then he noticed an odd-looking book, which he pulled out from the shelf. It was a photo album. Glancing at the closed bathroom door and hoping he had enough time, he peeked inside. There were photographs from Macy's childhood, cute photos, some were when she was missing teeth, and one with a pink bicycle helmet on her head. Then there were her school pictures from kindergarten through high school. He looked at each one, seeing how she'd grown from a cute little kid into a beautiful woman. He was very tempted to take a photo with him, but instead, he returned the book to its proper place.

Knocking on the bathroom door, he called, "You okay in there?"

"Yes, I'm just letting the hot water beat on me, washing away this entire night. I'm almost done. Just give me a minute and then you can come in." He heard the water turn off and he closed his eyes, leaning his forehead against the door. Just on the other side of the door, he knew, she was naked, and his body reacted to that knowledge. He kept repeating to himself that he was here to help her, but his little head was chanting, *Go, Go, Go.*

"I'm done. You can come in," Macy called. With that, Bryant turned the handle and pushed the door open. Macy sat on the edge of the tub, now wrapped up tightly in her robe. Her hair was wet, and her skin was fresh and clean. As he entered, she stood on her good foot and waited for him to carry her, but instead, he just stood in the doorway looking at her.

"You have no idea what a picture you make, with wet hair, in that robe, when I know you have nothing on under it."

"Bryant."

"Yeah?"

"Stop it. Don't look at me like that. I had a hard night."

"I'm having a hard night too, maybe a little different from yours, but definitely hard." When she realized what he was saying, he saw her eyes dart to his crotch, only making him harder. "Now you need to stop looking at me like that," he said. "Let's get you ready for bed, and you need to put the ice back on your ankle."

Macy wasn't thinking about her ankle at all. Actually, it wasn't hurting anymore. Standing in front of her was a very cute guy with a hard-on for her. She wanted to throw caution to the wind and jump him. She knew he wouldn't turn her down, but that stupid voice in her head kept telling her she shouldn't do it. Neither she nor Bryant moved. They just stared at one another, waiting.

Bryant finally broke the moment by saying her name again and stepping forward to carry her to her bedroom. Once he placed her on her bed, he left the room so she could get dressed. He had to get out of there, and he knew he needed to do it soon. He didn't want to leave her when he had no idea when he might see her again. He knew that if he stayed any longer, he would end up in her bed—not that it would have been a bad thing for him, but he didn't want her to regret it later. No, he didn't want that, and besides, he wanted more than just sex. He wanted to get to know her and to find out her likes and dislikes. He wanted to see if they had anything in common besides the physical attraction. He knew they both felt that.

"Bryant, you still out there?"

"Yeah, honey, I'm here. You need something?"

"Can you bring me out to the couch?"

Bryant opened her bedroom door and saw Macy sitting on her bed in a pair of silky pajamas. He tried not to look below her face. He needed to help her to the couch, and then go. His pants were already way too tight, and staying any longer certainly wouldn't help his situation. He sat Macy at one end of the couch and grabbed a blanket off the back to cover her. Maybe if he couldn't see her body, it would relieve some of his discomforts. However, when she patted the spot next to her, he knew relief wasn't going to come.

"Sit down with me a minute," she said. Bryant sat, being careful not to hit her ankle.

"Thank you for tonight," she said. "I know I imposed on you when I pulled you from your job and when you helped to get me out of the mess I made. I appreciate your helping me home. You went above and beyond anything I could have expected."

Bryant couldn't take hearing her praise any longer. "Macy, stop. I would have helped anyone in need, but you have to know how different you are from anybody else. When you kissed me at the pub, I felt something I've never felt before. My good deeds aren't with the purest of thoughts, because you know what you do to me. I had to try to not think about you naked in the shower, and then you asked me to go into your bedroom, and once again, I had to try not to imagine you in your bed. Don't get me wrong—I definitely want you, but not just for a one-night stand. Besides, I don't think casual flings are your thing. I understand that you want to concentrate on your career, and yet, I still want to be in your life."

"Bryant, if I thought that I could give you what you wanted and still advance in my job, believe me, you would be the man I'd choose. But as it is right now, I have to devote all of my time and energy to my job, and I don't think that would be fair to you. You should never have to be a second priority, but that's what would happen."

"Shh," Bryant said, "Right now you need to sleep, and I need to go. Thank you for the most amazing, craziest night." He kissed her on her forehead and got up. When he left the apartment, he locked the door behind him.

Bryant went down in the elevator knowing he'd done the right thing. Leaving Macy hadn't been easy but pushing her into something she wasn't ready for wouldn't do anybody any good. As he walked by the mailboxes again, he decided to take a better look. He found her apartment number, and there it was—her last name, Greene. Pulling his phone from his pocket, he typed all her information. She might be the investigative reporter, but Bryant could do a little of his own investigating to find out more about her.

Upstairs on the couch, Macy snuggled under the blanket, thinking about her night from hell. "Well, not all of it was bad," she said aloud. Thinking back to their first kiss, she thought about how she had been the aggressor. Never in her life had she done something like that—taking charge, kissing a man she didn't even know. She wasn't even sure if their kiss had anything to do with her fear of the goons who'd been chasing her. Although, she couldn't imagine those men doing anything bad to her in a crowded bar with Bryant by her side. He made her feel safe. So then, what had made her kiss him? And it hadn't been just any kiss. It was a hot-as-hell kiss. The kind that made her toes curl, a mind-numbing kiss, with no instinctual little voice in her head telling her not to do it.

Now, after the fact, she still wasn't sorry for kissing Bryant. Feeling his body close to hers had made her feel something she'd never felt before. She hated the fact that she couldn't start a relationship with him because she needed to focus on work. But the memory of that kiss would keep her mind occupied for a long time. Besides, she would have to see Bryant again when she returned Angela's clothes. Had she forgotten to give the outfit to him before he left, or had she done that on purpose? Underneath the cozy blanket, exhaustion started to take over, and Macy let her body relax. Tomorrow, she thought, she would…

Bryant drove back to the pub, wanting to make sure Paul had locked up. When he parked in the alley out back, he saw that Raylan's car was still there. Either Paul must have taken her home, or for some reason, she was still working. With the back door locked, Bryant thought at least if she was in the pub, she was safe. He hoped like hell they hadn't left Raylan to clean up alone. Unlocking the door, he heard voices. Who was still here? Sure enough, he saw the lights were on in the kitchen.

He saw a friend of Paul's, Jonathan Callahan, sitting on the counter while Raylan was giving him hell. Bryant stood still, so they didn't realize he was there. Raylan was moving around in the kitchen, slamming things. Bryant knew his sister's moods well. She liked to pout and stomp her feet, and it was all for show. When they were kids, she'd often used that same crap to get her way. Bryant wondered why she was mad at Jonathan. What did he do?

"I told you already that I'm not interested. Why do you keep coming back? I insult you, I call you names, and yet you won't go away."

"Ray, I don't think you really want me to go away. This is foreplay. You pretend not to like me, and then I chase you. It's a cat and mouse game."

"Get your butt off my clean counter and go away." She started pushing him off, but he grabbed her hand and pulled her between his legs.

"No can do. I promised your brother I would stay and make sure you made it to your car safely. Now we can talk about when we're going out for dinner?"

"Are you kidding me? I don't want to go out for dinner on my one night off. I want to sit in my pajamas and eat anything I don't have to make."

Bryant noticed Raylan wasn't trying to get away from Jonathan. Maybe something was going on between them.

"Ray, I'd make you dinner, and you can sit around in a sexy little teddy." That was when Raylan slapped him and backed away.

"Now that right there Jon is why I won't go out with you. You're a pig."

Bryant had heard enough, so he cleared his throat to get their attention. Both looked in his direction. "I'm glad you're not here alone because I would have to kick Paul's ass if he'd left you here." Stepping into the room, he watched Jonathan hop off the counter.

"How long have you been standing there eavesdropping?" Jonathan asked. Raylan's entire demeanor changed, and Bryant's curiosity piqued about her and Jonathan's friend-relationship. Jonathan was a good guy, but if his sister didn't want him around, Bryant would make it clear Jon needed to back off.

"Long enough, Jon," Bryant said as he lifted his chin in greeting. "What's going on Ray?"

"Nothing Bry, what's going on with you? What happened with that woman, and why didn't you come back to close up? Oh, I know—you got laid." He knew what she was doing, shifting the attention to him rather than answering his unasked question.

"No." Bryant didn't want Raylan thinking he took Macy home to have sex with her.

Now Jonathan chimed in, "Damn, you struck out."

Bryant looked at him, and said again, "No."

"Bro, either you got laid, or you struck out, there is no in between."

Bryant didn't want to explain anything in front of Jonathan but avoiding the question would just make things worse. "I had to park two blocks from her place, and she twisted her ankle walking in Angela's shoes."

"Oh man," Jonathan said, "that sucks. No wonder you didn't get laid."

"Again, you're such a pig, Jonathan. That's all you ever have on your mind."

"Come on, Ray. All guys want to get laid, right Bry?"

"Don't drag me into this. I like Macy, and I'd like to get to know her better, but she wants to concentrate on her job and doesn't have time for a relationship. Not that that's going to stop me."

Bryant was already thinking about a way to see her again. Maybe he would bring her dinner, especially with her twisted ankle. He wanted her off her feet. He didn't know whether she worked on Saturdays, and he had a crew working in the morning. It was rare for Bryant to take a day off, but tomorrow might be one of those days. If that was the case, then he needed to get some sleep.

"Ray, are you almost done here? Jonathan, you can take off. I'll stay with my sister and see her safely to her car."

"Uh, um, I don't mind staying with her." Jonathan stammered. Bryant could see his discomfort.

"Don't fight over me, boys, I'm ready to go anyway. We can all walk out together, just as soon as I wipe his butt print off my counter." After swiping a cleaning cloth over the spot Jonathan had just vacated, Raylan grabbed her purse.

Once they were out the door, Bryant turned to Jonathan and said, "Thanks for staying with her." The two men shook hands, but Bryant could feel the tension coming from the other man as they watched Raylan walk to her car.

"Yeah, anytime," Jonathan said. Bryant stood still, held his spot until Jonathan turned to walk away.

"Night, Ray," Jonathan called. Raylan waved and unlocked her car. "Night, Jon."

Bryant wanted to make sure his sister was comfortable with Jonathan staying with her. "Hold up," he called as she got into her car. If she didn't feel comfortable, he would talk to Paul about it.

"Bryant, it's been a long night, I just want to go home and shower."

"This is just going to take a minute. Are you okay with Jon hanging out with you like that, because if you're not, I'll tell Paul to talk to him?"

"I don't need help from you or Paul. I hate to tell you this, but I can take care of myself. Jonathan wouldn't try anything, because he knows Paul would kill him if he did. Jonathan is looking for one thing, and he's not going to find it here. I am not one of his many conquests, and I will not be the topic of the pub or firehouse gossip."

"I don't think Paul would allow that either."

"Just leave it alone, okay? And thanks for talking to Paul about the phone tonight. He can be a big pain in the butt, even though I know he'll always have my back."

"We all will, even when you're the one who's being the pain in the butt." He kissed the top of her head. "I'll wait until you pull out. And drive safe—there are a lot of drunks on the road." He watched as she got into her old clunker. She refused to buy a new car and drive it in the city. Their dad made sure her car was always in good working order, but still you never really knew when it might decide not to start. Moving to his truck, Bryant realized he was exhausted, and he still had a forty-five-minute drive home.

{5}

Bryant bought an old house right outside of the city. It was something he worked on when he had time. He'd wanted a house with space, a place he could grow into with land, and trees. With the late hour or early, depending on how you looked at it, the roads had no traffic. The stretch of road on the way out of the city gave Bryant time to think about Macy and that kiss. The way her body struggled to get close to his, and the way his body had reacted to hers. He was no altar boy, at least he hadn't been in a long time. As he had admitted to Macy, he had many impure thoughts about her. He didn't want to rush in and give her the wrong idea. Yes, he wanted to be with her, but it wasn't only about that.

There was just something about her, and he couldn't quite put his finger on it. It was something about how she made him feel, how he responded to her scent, her smile. When was the last time he had paid that much attention to the way a woman smelled? Yeah, maybe he noticed when they wore some fancy fragrance, but with Macy, it was different. It was her natural aroma, a perfume all her own that attracted him to her. Then there were her brown eyes—big, expressive eyes that at first, were hidden behind her dark-rimmed glasses. He hadn't even thought to ask her if she needed the glasses to see. Although she had seemed to manage without them, he would make sure she got them back.

He thought about how she looked in her work clothes, the plain dress, and jacket that had made her look so out of place at the punk rock show at the pub. Then he thought about her in Angela's clothes. She had changed from librarian to a wildcat, not that he thought she had been comfortable in that outfit—far from it. When he thought how the dress hugged her curves, he said aloud, "God I'm sorry, but she was hot. I know I shouldn't be lusting after her, but I'm just a man. I'm a big fat pig, as Raylan would say, just like the rest of the entire male species." He had to laugh at his thoughts.

When Macy woke, her ankle was throbbing, reminding her that last night wasn't a bad dream. Taking a deep breath, she tried to sit up to look at her ankle, hoping that it wasn't as bad as it felt. She pulled the blanket back to look, and sure enough, a purple and swollen ankle greeted her. She slid her good foot to the floor, thinking that putting weight on her bad ankle wasn't a good idea. Coffee—she had to have coffee. But how was she going to get to the kitchen or the bathroom? With that thought, she had to go, bad. Slipping onto the floor, she began to crawl. "There is no shame in doing what you have to do," Macy said to herself.

On the way out of the bathroom, she passed her little office and spotted her desk chair, which had wheels. "Yes, I can make that work."

There was no way she was leaving the house today. She would have to work from home, and if she wasn't going out, then she could stay in her PJs. She didn't bother to brush her hair or clean her face. She wheeled herself into the kitchen to make coffee, and get an ice pack, and then she rolled herself to her computer. After wrapping her ankle in plastic wrap to keep the ice in place, the way Bryant had done, she pulled out a deck drawer to rest her leg on, and then she took two pain pills so she could focus on her work.

For hours, Macy searched the internet, trying to locate the owners of the clubs where the six underage girls had gone missing. Each time she thought she found something it turned out to be a dead end. She searched public records for "Jim Smith," but none of the names matched the man from the nightclub. She even Googled Mr. Smith, and again, got nothing useful. That alone set off all kinds of warning bells. She couldn't even find a picture of the man, though guys who looked like Mr. Smith always loved to have their picture taken. And yet, she found no press photos, no beautiful woman on his arm, no social event, nothing.

What she did find were hundreds of pictures that people had posted to social media from the various clubs. She knew she was looking for a needle in a haystack, but she combed through each picture, looking for one of the girls in the background. Lucky for her, with the posts dated, she didn't have to look through every picture. Macy couldn't even prove the girls had been in the clubs when they'd disappeared. Without the surveillance tapes, she could only go by the witness statements.

Macy was engrossed in her work and didn't realize she hadn't eaten until her stomach made a very unladylike noise. She needed to give her eyes a rest anyway, so she pushed her chair towards the kitchen. She was rolling down the hall when her door buzzer went off. Looking at her door, she debated whether she should answer. The buzzer went off again, and this time she heard Bryant's voice, "Macy? It's Bryant O'Shea." She took a deep breath and rolled to the door so she could push the intercom button to speak to him.

"Bryant, what are you doing here?" Looking down at herself, she wanted to kick her butt for not getting dressed—or at least brushing her hair.

"I wanted to check on you, and I brought you dinner." The mention of food had her hitting the buzzer to unlock the outside door. If he had to wait for the elevator, then she would have about five minutes to get ready before he'd reach her door. Macy rushed into the bathroom as fast as the chair would allow her to go. She grabbed her hairbrush off the sink, wildly attempting to brush her hair and teeth at the same time. Just as she spit out the toothpaste, her doorbell rang.

Macy rolled the chair to the door and unlocked it for Bryant. Her heart beat fast, and her breath rushed out when she opened the door and saw him. Bryant leaned against her doorjamb with two big bags hanging from each hand. He looked so good, with his dark blue shirt that stretched across his hard chest, and jeans that hugged his hips.

He started to say, "You shouldn't be on your…" but when he saw her in the chair, he started to laugh. "Here I was thinking you were helpless all day, not being able to get around. I should have known you'd figure out a way." He stepped inside, shutting the door behind him. "How's the ankle today?"

"Not my best day, but I made it work. Getting to the bathroom this morning wasn't pretty," she said as he pushed her into the kitchen.

"You hungry? I didn't know what you like so I brought a little bit of everything." Sitting the bags on her counter, he unloaded them. "I have Chinese, burgers, or sub-sandwiches. What's your pleasure?" Turning to look at her, he was surprised to see a little mischievous glow in her eyes.

"Surprise me, but let's eat in the living room. Plates are in that cabinet," Macy pointed and rolled herself into the other room as she heard Bryant moving around in her kitchen.

Bryant was surprised how easily Macy allowed him to waltz in and serve her dinner. He had thought he'd have to convince her to open the door, or that he'd have to wait out front until he could follow someone else into the building. He was shocked when Macy buzzed him in and even more so when he hadn't had to fight with her to open the apartment door. Now here he was putting food on a plate for her.

Using several plates, he laid out all the food. That way he couldn't go wrong. In the living room, he set the dishes on the table in front of her, and then carefully he took a seat next to her so he wouldn't disturb her ankle. When he'd seen her in the computer chair, he should have known she'd find some way to manage, and he was glad to see she'd kept ice on it. Just as he was thinking how nice it would be, having dinner sitting next to her, she broke the silence first.

"Bryant, why are you here? I know you said you were checking on me," she motioned her hand over all the food sitting on the table, "but all this food? That's more than just making sure I'm alright."

"I know, but I wasn't sure if you could get around enough to make something to eat. What kind of guy would I be if I weren't worried that you might starve to death? Besides, I wanted to know if your ankle had gotten any worse, or if you needed to see a doctor. I didn't know if you had someone who could take you if you needed to go." He tried not to sound too desperate, but he wanted to see her again.

Just then, Macy's stomach rumbled loudly, and she took a plate off her coffee table. "You were right about one thing—I'm starving, but not because I couldn't fix something to eat. I was working, and I forgot to eat. I was wheeling into the kitchen when you hit my buzzer downstairs, and when you mentioned food I couldn't resist," Macy said, taking a bite out of the big burger in her fist.

"I see. So, it was the food that got me through the door, and here I thought it was me. I knew it was too easy. I expected either a fight or a whole lot of convincing to get me through your door again. Well, at least I'm feeding you. Now you can tell me about how your ankle feels, and how you managed to work today." He took one of the plates from the table and started in on his food as he kept his eyes on her.

"I couldn't go into work, so I was working from home. I know it's not broken, because I think I'd be in more pain. Although, it is a pretty color purple. I've taken pain meds every few hours when I remembered to take them. That's how I know it's just sprained, and nothing more serious, because if the pain didn't sidetrack me from my work, then it must be fine, right? I've also been a good girl and remembered to put the ice on it. I'll be fine. It was stupid of me to think I could walk more than a few steps, much less two blocks in those shoes. Which reminds me, I have Angela's clothes, and I need my stuff back. My glasses are what I need back the most. I have an old pair that I can use for now." She pushed the glasses up on her face, as they fell down her nose.

Bryant watched Macy as she spoke, her eyes were so expressive. She talked almost as if she was thinking aloud. He liked listening to her and seeing how animated her hands were as she went on, moving from one subject to the next without any confirmation from him. When she noticed him watching her, she stopped talking. He wanted her to continue, so he looked down at his burger and pretended he hadn't been studying her.

"I am going to get my stuff back, right? I paid a lot of money for those glasses." She watched his reaction, to see if he was going to comply with her request to get her belongings back.

Reaching into the pocket of his hoodie, he pulled free her eyeglasses. "I should have given them to you the moment I walked through the door, but I was caught up in the fact that you didn't battle with me, I forgot I had them." Taking them, she held them to her chest, as if hugging them. The movement drew his attention to her breasts, and he noticed that she wasn't wearing a bra. She was still in the silk pajamas from last night, and the thoughts that followed had the same effect on him as they had the night before. How he hadn't noticed it before, he didn't know.

When she threw her arms around him in a hug, his mind went straight to stripping the silk from her body. Her hair was still a mess from sleep, and she had no makeup on, but to him she was beautiful. Just the fact that she felt comfortable with him seeing her not at her best and the fact that she didn't care if she wasn't all put together, appealed to him. This was the real her, not someone phony.

Macy pulled back from the hug too soon before he was ready to let go.

"Thank you, thank you so much," she smiled at him, still clutching the glasses.

"Macy," he paused, trying to make sure his words were right before he said anything wrong. "I like you. I know what you said about concentrating on work. I understand that, but I can't help wanting to spend time with you, the way we are right now. We both work, so, why can't we fill the rest of the time with each other? I don't see how it could hurt to watch a movie together or sit here and have dinner like we are now. What do you say?"

He was hoping she would agree with him and then they could spend some time together as they got to know one another. He could see Macy was going to turn him down, but she didn't say anything, and it was making him uncomfortable. He didn't want her to say no, but the fact that she was so quiet had him not knowing where he stood.

Macy sat stock-still, stunned by his insistence that they date. Here she was, reveling in Bryant's company, doing the exact thing, she knew she shouldn't be doing—leading him on and sending mixed signals. It's just that she found him easy to talk to and to be around. He almost made her forget the promise she'd made to herself because work had to come first. She didn't have time for a relationship, or time for him, although the thought of sending Bryant away made her chest hurt.

Bryant asked, "Macy, are you still with me?" She could see him looking at her.

"Bryant, I like you too… but I'm not going to have every night off as you do. I don't work a nine-to-five job. For this story I'm doing, I have to work during the day searching for clues, and at night I have to investigate those nightclubs or wherever they take me."

"Like you did last night? And you ended up having two goons following you? It's not safe for you to be out there alone with no backup. What would have happened if I hadn't helped you?"

She could see he wasn't happy with her statement about doing her job. She couldn't blame him. And she truly didn't know what would have happened to her if he hadn't stepped in and helped.

"I don't think they wanted to hurt me. I think that maybe those men wanted to scare me a little or find out more about me, what paper I work for and where I live. As I said, I didn't tell anyone my real name or where I work. Their boss accused me of working for one of the missing girls' families."

"Missing girls? What missing girls?" Bryant asked. *Oh crap*, she thought, *I just let the cat out of the bag.*

"Six under-aged girls showed fake IDs to get into six different clubs, months apart. Then those six girls disappeared. The police didn't think their cases were connected," she made air quotes, "They classified them all as runaways. I think there are too many coincidences for all of them to be runaways. I looked over each police report, but there wasn't much to go by, so I'm doing some digging of my own."

Bryant frowned, "How did you manage to look at the reports from the police?"

"Look, I've already told you too much. I have to take a shower now. Thank you for dinner." When she started to move towards her rolling chair, Bryant stopped her.

It seemed just to hit him what she was working on, "Wait just a minute. Are you telling me you're investigating six missing girls from nightclubs?"

"Yes."

"Oh, shit. Macy, this could be dangerous, and I don't think you should keep poking around."

Macy couldn't believe what she was hearing—this man, whom she'd only met last night, wanted to try to tell her what to do? Knowing her temper, she told herself she wasn't going to fight with him about her job. Bryant had a lot of nerve thinking he had any right to press his opinion about what she should or shouldn't do. "Lock up after you leave," she said, keeping her tone even. She transferred her body into the computer chair and rolled toward the bathroom. With any luck, Bryant would be gone by the time she got out. She didn't need a man telling her what to do, even if he was cute, and even if she had dreamt about him last night, he had to go.

Bryant sat watching her roll away from him, stunned. When she shut the bathroom door, he recovered his senses and realized she was kicking him out. But he wasn't done with her, not by a long shot. Without thinking, he went for the bathroom door and reached for the handle. Opening the door, he said, "Macy, we are not—" but Bryant stopped in his tracks. Just inside the bathroom door, Macy was standing on her good foot, naked. "Oh, shit, I'm sorry."

"Hey, what the hell are you doing?" Macy stood clutching her silk pajama top to her chest.

His actions dumbfounded and overwhelmed him because she stood there holding her shirt against her body, that didn't cover much. He shouldn't have followed her. Immediately, Bryant turned his back, but the image of her naked body ingrained in his head. Damn, that two-second glance he'd taken before she covered herself had his mind scrambled. "I'm sorry. I didn't think you had gotten undressed yet."

"GET OUT."

Behind him, Bryant could hear her scurrying into the shower to hide behind the curtain. Smiling to himself, he waited until he heard the shower curtain close, before turning back around.

"Macy," he said her name in a calming voice.

"NO. Don't you 'Macy' me. Get out of my bathroom, out of my apartment, and out of my life, Bryant O'Shea. I do not need a man telling me what to do, much less a man I met yesterday. You have seen more of me in one day than any other stranger I've known for less than twenty-four hours. Get out, lock the door, and stop smiling!"

"How do you know I'm smiling?"

"I can feel it that's how. This is so unfair, because you've seen me in that awful dress that didn't cover much at all, and as humiliating as I thought that was, now you've seen me naked. Man, my life keeps getting better and better," Macy said bitterly.

"Hell, my life is getting better and better. And I don't think you should feel ashamed. You have a beautiful body. I know—I saw it, even though it was just a brief glimpse. If being naked was so embarrassing and unfair, well, I could always get naked too and join you… just to be fair and all. I've seen you, so now you could see me."

The room became completely silent. Macy didn't immediately oppose his suggestion. Did that mean she was thinking about his proposition? God, he hoped so. The suspense was killing him. Bryant realized he wasn't even breathing.

"As much as I might enjoy you joining me, I don't think it's a good idea. It would be sending mixed messages, more than I already have. I can't have someone looking over my shoulder all the time or telling me what to do. I can take care of myself just fine."

"I'm sorry. I don't know what came over me, Macy. Well, actually, that's not true. I do know. I don't want to see you get hurt. I know what you're doing is important, but having two guys following you… I have to say…I don't like it. Now, before you say anything else, just listen, okay?" Macy didn't say anything, so Bryant continued, "I know I have no right to tell you what to do, and I don't mean to come across as overbearing, but ever since I laid eyes on you, I have felt very protective of you. I know it hasn't even been a whole day since we met, but I can't just turn and walk away. When you kissed me in the pub, you flicked a switch in me, and now I can't get you out of my head. Can we find a middle ground, a compromise? I could go with you at night when you investigate and protect you."

"Bryant, I can't let you get involved."

"I hate to tell you this Macy, but it's too late. I'm already involved. And I'm tired of talking to you through this curtain. It's your choice—you can come out, or I'm coming in. You have two seconds to make up your mind."

{6}

Before Macy could say anything, Bryant had already removed his clothes and stepped into the small shower. She stood there in disbelief, with the end of the shower curtain draped in front of her body.

When she regained her voice, she said, "You have no boundaries. No sense of personal space." Her eyes stayed on his, even if she wanted to look down.

"Now we're even. Look all you want. My body does not embarrass me. I hope looking at me will make you feel the same need that I have been feeling for you." He watched as her sultry eyes finally swept down his body. Every masculine bone in his body tingled. He could feel his muscles twitching as her eyes raked over his skin.

"I... Bryant... You are gorgeous. I wouldn't be embarrassed either if I had your body. I would be advertising underwear. Women would buy them just to look at you. Holy crap."

When he started to step towards her, he saw Macy's eyes grow huge. She was clutching the shower curtain for dear life. "Bryant."

"Yes, Macy?" He stopped with just inches between them. Taking her head in his hands, looking into her eyes, he said, "Tell me you don't want this."

"I, um, I just don't know you well enough. Not that my body isn't saying, 'Yes please,'" Macy's voice came out as a high-pitched squeak.

"Fair enough, but just know I'm not backing away." He pressed his lips to hers and felt her body relax into his. Even with the thin fabric of the curtain between them, he could feel her heat.

Macy couldn't help deepening the kiss. When they kissed, she felt she lost all control. With the curtain forgotten, her arm came up around Bryant's neck. He pressed her into the shower wall, and she arched into him. As she felt his hardness against her abdomen, and his hands roaming down her body, Macy's mind stopped thinking, and her body tingled with a deep sensation. He pulled back, too soon, and a disapproving noise escaped her lips.

"Macy, I don't want to push you into anything you're not ready for."

"I hate to tell you this, but I think it might be too late," she said. Macy kissed Bryant again, and he let out a groan.

Bryant knew he should pull back. That if he rushed her now, she would regret it later. But having her naked and pressed against him in her shower had his body urging him onward. He had to slow things down. Pulling back again, he asked, "Can I wash you, Macy? Nothing more for tonight it will be us just getting to know one other."

When Bryant saw Macy nod, he reached for the water. The cold water hit his back, taking his breath away for a moment before he felt it cool his overheated skin. He turned Macy as the water became warm and watched as she stood under the steady stream and tried his best not to overreact to her being so close and so naked.

Macy lifted her hands to wet her hair, closing her eyes as the water cascaded down her back. Her breasts pressed out as she arched her back. His hands wanted to touch her, but he balled them into fists instead. Watching her was like an exotic fantasy—a dream where he could only look at her but couldn't touch.

Macy's eyes opened, and she took his hand in her own. She opened her shampoo, not saying a word, and poured a small amount into his open palm. Rubbing his hands together, he made a lather of the soap and started washing her hair. Her eyes closed again while his fingers massaged her scalp. Macy made approving sounds, and he could have sworn that the noises went straight to his already-aroused body parts. As he worked his fingers through her hair, her body pressed up against his. Feeling her breasts and her hard nipples rubbing along his chest hair had his breathing coming out in short spurts.

"Mumm, I've never had a man wash my hair before. You must have had a lot of practice because you're very good at it."

"Nope, this is my first time," he said and leaned her back so she could rinse the shampoo. "I like it, though. A lot. Do I get to wash anything else?"

Wordlessly, Macy took his hand and poured body soap into it. Then she took another bottle, conditioner, and stroked it into her hair. He knew his hands would soon be on her body. They trembled as he worked the body wash back and forth in his palms.

He started with her shoulders, rubbing, and massaging as he went, working his hands down over her arms and back up again. Then he turned her so he could wash her back. Looking down at her butt, he had to swallow hard. When he'd finished with her back, Bryant moved his hands slowly over each cheek, squeezing and kneading her flesh. She bent over, resting her hands on the shower wall. He thought he might lose it. Slowly he crouched so he could wash her legs, which brought his eyes level with her butt. She opened her legs, and he nearly had a heart attack.

"Macy, do you have any idea how beautiful you are? I mean, damn. You have absolutely no reason to be embarrassed because if you could see yourself through my eyes... I have to tell you this might have been the dumbest idea I've ever had. Now that I've touched you, and now that I know what I know, there is no going back." He stood and turned her to face him and kissed her.

"You haven't finished yet. You didn't do my front."

"Yeah, well, I'm afraid to touch you there."

"Afraid? Why?" Her dark chocolate eyes sparkled.

"If I touch you anywhere near your chest, I won't be able to stop at just washing your body."

Macy laughed and took the soap, lathering it in her hands as he watched. She washed the rest of her body, moving her hands over her breasts and all the way down to her belly, then turning to give him a full view. At this point, he understood what she'd been doing—torturing him with his own dumb idea. It wasn't until she grabbed the soap again and put more into her hands that he realized she, wasn't done.

"Your turn now, and if you think I'm going to take it easy on you, you can forget it." She started on his broad shoulders. As she worked the soap over them, she said, "Next time you think about invading my personal space, you might want to think again. Because now you know how it will backfire on you. I plan on touching every square inch of you."

Macy planned to inflict the harshest punishment he could ever imagine. Her hands played over his body, moving, and squeezing, and she was enjoying every minute of it. He wanted to allow her to have her fun, and it served him right for getting in there with her, but hell, he wasn't going be able to take much more of this before his hands would be on her. When her hand moved south, and she took him in her fist, his head hit the shower wall. Nope, his body couldn't take it.

"Macy honey, if you keep that up I'm going to come."

She laughed. "We can't have that, now can we?"

His eyes flew open. He couldn't stand the tease. All bets were off. His hands found her waist, and he pulled her into him, stopping her hand from moving. He wanted her—even as needy as he felt he knew she had all the control.

"Now, Bryant, you're not going back on your word, are you? Just washing, nothing else, you said. I can't help it if you didn't take full advantage of your turn. Remember, you said you were afraid to touch me." He stared open-mouthed. She dared to bat her eyelashes at him.

"I was trying to be a gentleman and not take advantage of you."

"Uh, first of all, I don't think a gentleman would have just walked in on a woman taking a shower and secondly, a nobleman wouldn't force his way into her shower. You play a good part, Bryant O'Shea, but you don't fool me—you are no gentleman."

"Oh, I can be a gentleman. You want to watch me stop this and walk out? Because I can. I'll prove I am a gentleman." He needed to regain control of the situation.

"No, I don't, but I think I proved my point." She moved the curtain and stepped out of the tub and fell. She'd forgotten about her ankle. Now she was on the floor naked, laughing at the picture she knew she must have made with her arm draped over her face.

"Damn Macy, are you, all right?" Bryant leaped out of the shower after her.

Macy rolled to her side, still laughing so hard she snorted. Feeling Bryant's hands examining her ankle, she said, "Well that didn't turn out to be to such a grand exit, did it?" She realized what she must look like and tried to cover her nude body.

"I just hope you're alright," he said, looking at the deep purple bruises. "I hope you didn't make it worse with this fall."

"Can you pass me my robe, please?" He watched as she shrugged into her cover, hiding her body from his view.

"Feeling a little modest now that you're not proving your point, hmm?" Bryant asked. "When we were in the shower, you had everything out there, and now you want to hide." Bryant moved his finger down the opening of her robe and Macy slapped his hand away.

"See, a gentleman would not point that out." Macy tried to get up and failed. Bryant stood and picked her up right off the floor as if she weighed nothing. Carrying her to the bedroom, he put her in the middle of the bed and left the room and returned with a towel for her.

Bryant sat on the side of the bed. He hunched over, resting his arms on his thighs. "Macy, I'm not going to pretend that I don't want you, because we both know that I do. But I think that the feeling is mutual unless you tell me otherwise. You drive me crazy. I want you, of course, but most of all I want your safety. I don't want to get in the way of you doing your job, but I do want you protected. Yes, I know, we haven't even known each other for more than one whole day yet, but I want to have the chance to get to know you. This isn't just about getting into your bed, Macy."

"Bryant, look, I'm not sure I even have anything to offer you. I'm not going to lie and say that I don't enjoy spending time with you. I just showered with you, for God's sake, and that shower was more intimate than most sex I've had. I've never had a man make me feel important the way you do. I don't plan to get all mushy on you, so don't be scared that I think you could be my prince charming. I'm just not the type of girl to have friends with benefits."

"Macy, I told you this isn't just about sex. Can we try to see if you can do both, date, and work? I don't care if we spend the night in the car scoping out leads. If I get to spend time with you and keep you safe in the meantime, then I think that's a win-win."

"You really wouldn't mind sitting in a car all night doing nothing but people watching? See, I don't know too many guys that want to do that night after night."

"Well, there you have it. I do want to do it, and if it gives us time to talk, or maybe leads to a little kissing, how could I say no to that?" Bryant moved his brows up and down.

Shaking her head, Macy said, "Against my better judgment, we will try. But you can't get in the way of me doing my job," she put her hands on her hips.

Bryant was happy with the turn of events. All he'd had to do was convince her that spending time together didn't have to interfere with her work. He was looking forward to helping her on the job because if it came down to her safety, he would be doing a hell of a lot more than just "getting in the way."

First, he wanted to apologize for invading her privacy. "We need to talk about what happened in the shower. Well, not just the shower, but the bathroom in general. I'm sorry that I barged in on you, and then pushed my way into your shower. I'm sorry, I made you feel the need to have the last word, and that you fell out of the tub." Bryant started to snicker but quickly tried to hide his laughter.

Macy knew he'd stopped being serious about halfway through his apology. "What?" she asked. "You might need to put your clothes back on, Mr. O'Shea, because I'm thinking you may need another lesson—on how to be humble in defeat."

He laughed, but he wasn't thinking about her words. He thought that she could teach him a few things about how it would feel to be killed with pleasure. One day he would get to take all of that passion she had to give, and when that day came, he would relish it, and he would give her more than she ever expected. He couldn't wait.

The next day was a Sunday, and Bryant rushed to get to church. In his family, no one missed church unless they had no other option, like when his brother was working a shift at the firehouse, or when someone was running a fever. And yes, his mother would come over to check on you and make sure you were legitimately absent from church.

Although it was frowned upon when people stepped through the doors just as the ushers were closing them for Mass, Bryant made it in for the service at the last moment. He took his seat at the end of the family pew, right in front, where they had been sitting ever since Bryant could remember. His mother didn't look up at him, but he knew she was aware of the time. As soon as he sat down the music started, and then his Uncle Joe, known as Father O'Shea by everyone else, walked down the aisle. Uncle Joe zeroed in on Bryant, smiling. He knew that smile meant to see his uncle after Mass. How could Uncle Joe know already? Was it that obvious that Bryant had fallen for someone? Or maybe Ray had blabbed to the family already?

When it was time to receive communion, Bryant avoided his family and got in the other line. As he made his way to the front of the church, his uncle just smiled at him and shook his head. When he was within earshot, Uncle Joe said, "See me before you run off today. It will only take a minute," then just like that, he went back to giving out the Eucharist. It had to have been Raylan who ratted on him, or maybe it had been Tane?

When Bryant returned to the pew, his sisters were whispering amongst themselves. As he sat, their mother gave the girls a meaningful look, and they fell silent. Now, Bryant had no doubt, whatever his uncle wanted to talk to him about had something to do with what happened on Friday night. If Raylan's mouth was the reason for all the gossip, well, she'd better watch out because he could start spreading his own rumors. It was childish, he knew, but somehow his siblings brought that out of him.

As Mass ended, Bryant's mother confronted him. "You were late this morning. Anything I need to know about?"

"Nope, just slept through my alarm," he said casually. Thank God, it was true because lying to his mother was never a good idea. Arlene O'Shea could smell the fear in her children when they lied. As Bryant became older, he'd learned that if his mother asking him a question. Then she already knew the answer. She nodded her head, as she looked him over. He couldn't tell what she was thinking, but he didn't like the way she studied him. Thankfully, one of the ladies from her church group interrupted them and saved Bryant from any more scrutiny. Releasing a breath, he thought, one down and one still to go. As always, his Uncle Joe stood at the doorway talking to everyone and shaking hands as his congregation left. Bryant waited for his uncle at the top of the stairs, knowing they would go into his office behind the church for their private talk.

Sunday was the day Macy liked to catch up on her household chores. She did all her cleaning, dusting, and vacuuming. Even with her ankle feeling better the tasks were still hard. She put off doing laundry until she could figure how to get to the elevator and down to the basement while carrying her dirty clothes. She stripped her sheets off and shoved them into her pillowcase, throwing the bundle out into the hallway. Hobbling around the bed, she put clean sheets on her bed. She was out of breath by the time she finished the task. Macy dusted her nightstand and vacuumed the room from where she sat on the side of her bed. Anything she couldn't reach from there would have to wait until next week's Sunday cleaning when her ankle felt better.

She vacuumed the living room while sitting in her computer chair. She knew it looked silly, but it worked. Exhausted, Macy lay on her couch, closing her eyes just for a minute. A loud buzzing noise sounded from far away, she wondered, *where is that coming from*? As her mind cleared, she realized it was her door buzzer. It had to be either her parents or Bryant. She didn't feel like getting up and answering her door, no matter who was there. Then his voice came over the intercom's speaker.

"Macy? I know you're there, so buzz me in, and I'll show you what I brought you today."

"You weak, weak woman," she said to herself as she moved to the door so she could buzz him in and unlock the front door. She stood waiting for him and watched through her peephole until he came into view. He carried bags in each hand, as he had the previous night, but tonight they didn't look like takeout food bags. Taking a moment to look him over through the peephole, she saw that he wore a golf shirt with his construction company's logo on it and jeans.

"Macy, open up." Bryant stood there looking so damned cute. His face had a little scruff around his chin. He said, "I can see your shadow. I know you're staring at me through the peephole." His face moved until it came close to the door and he smiled.

"You cannot see me, no way," she stepped back.

"I can see you when you put your face against the hole to see out. That's why if anyone comes to your door and you didn't buzz them in, don't look through the peephole, because then they know your home."

She opened the door for him. He kissed her as he walked in. Tonight, he put the bags on the table in the living room. Turning to face her, he asked, "How's the ankle today?"

"I can put some pressure on it, but I think I overdid it today when I was cleaning," she said as she limped to the sofa. "I still haven't figured out how to get my laundry done. I can't carry the baskets to the elevator, much less into the basement."

"I can help you after I show you what I brought today," he sounded all excited. "I stopped by a buddy of mine's shop and bought you a bunch of spy equipment. Look, I have night goggles and a spy camera," he said as he was taking stuff out of the bag, "and here's a recording pen— no one will even know you're recording them. It has really good sound quality. You can even have it in your purse, and its sound activated with a tracking device. And here's a panic button you can put on your keychain if you find yourself in a situation where you need to get someone's attention, push the button. It's loud. And an alarm for your door. I even bought bugs for you to plant. If you have a chance to get inside one of the clubs again, you could plant one of these buggers."

"Wait, Bryant, this stuff must have cost a fortune. I can't pay you for all this. As cool as this stuff is, I can't afford it. I hope you can return it."

"Don't worry about it. As I said, my buddy owns the shop, and believe me he owes me big time. He was happy that he could help me out. His place has high-tech stuff, but most people go to him for baby cams, or stuff to help them spy on their cheating spouses. Private investigators get their stuff from him too, so I don't see why an investigative journalist shouldn't have access to the same things for her investigations."

"I still can't pay you, no matter how great everything is."

He stopped her from talking by kissing her, pulling her into him. "Macy, I don't want you to pay me back. I want you to be safe. If sneaking around at nightclubs and doing dangerous interviews is what you have to do, then I want to do everything I can to ensure you get your story and get out safely."

Macy had never met anyone like Bryant, and his actions confused her. Yesterday he said he didn't want her poking around at all, and then today he buys out everything from some spy place. As much as she would have loved to use the new equipment he'd brought, she couldn't just accept that kind of gift—especially from a man she hadn't even gone on a date, nor had sex with even if they did come close to it yesterday.

"Macy, I can hear you thinking, debating with yourself. Come on. I want you to have this stuff. I was so excited to show it to you, and now you're thinking about not accepting it."

"How do you know that I'm not going to take all this stuff and run? Besides, I don't like how quickly you get into my head. Don't think you know me."

He smiled, "I hate to tell you this, Macy, but you are not hard to read. Your eyes give you away. They're very expressive. So, don't ever try playing poker, because you have tells," he laughed.

"I do not."

"Let's get your laundry started downstairs and then we can start playing with all this equipment." Bryant was truly excited, like a big kid on Christmas morning.

{7}

Bryant carried Macy's two baskets of clothing and linens to the elevator and helped her hobble down the hall at the same time. The elevator didn't go all the way down to the basement, so they had to walk down one flight of stairs. Bryant gave her a piggyback ride down the steps, enjoying the feeling of her legs wrapped tight around his waist, and her arms around his neck.

They started a couple of loads of wash, and since there was no way she would leave her clothes unattended because someone would steal them, he propped her up on a washer. This position put her at just the right height for him to step between her legs. He talked about all the crazy things he found in his friend's spy shop. As he talked, she took the opportunity to examine every aspect of his face. She looked at the little creases near the corners of his amazing blue-green eyes, at his high cheekbones and strong jaw, dusted with the beginnings of a reddish beard. She wanted to run her hands over it, to see if it felt as soft as it looked.

His shoulders were broad and strong, most likely from working construction all day, and so was his chest. Which she personally knew had some reddish hair—hair that was just enough to entice her into his happy little trail that ran down past his flat, tight abs. He had a killer smile, with perfect white teeth. He was flashing her that smile now.

"Macy, have you heard one word I've said?" He put his fingers under her chin to tilt her face up to his.

"Nope, I was busy looking at you. You can be very distracting, you know." Here she was, sitting on a washing machine with this gorgeous guy in front of her, and she was just a Plain Jane kind of girl. What did he see when he looked at her? She had straight brown hair and wore glasses. She looks more like a librarian than a natural beauty. There wasn't much about her that she considered beautiful. She didn't even have straight teeth, because she'd refused to wear her retainer when she was a kid. Macy hadn't really ever questioned her appearance before. While she knew that she wasn't ugly by any means, she'd never had anyone look at her the way Bryant did.

"What are you thinking about in that head of yours? I can see the wheels spinning. You want to share?"

"Not really, but I am trying to figure you out. I mean, we just met two days ago, and yet you seem as comfortable with me as if we've known each other for years. You buy me hundreds of dollars' worth of stuff, but yet, you say you're looking for nothing in return. Sorry if I'm confused, but most people aren't like you. Most people act a certain way until they get what they want, and then they revert to being assholes. I'm just not sure if you're too good to be true. Before I start falling for you, I'd like to know who you are."

"Actually, it's funny you should say that. I wasn't sure how to bring this up, but now that you've mentioned that you want to know who I am. I know this is going to sound weird, but my uncle is a priest and he wants to meet you. He is someone you can ask and know you're getting an honest answer."

"Why does he want to meet me? How does he even know about me? I mean, did you tell him, why would you tell him about me?"

"Calm down, Macy. I didn't tell him, but I'm sure my sister or brother did. They're big tattletales, every last one of them." Macy laughed at his expression. "After Mass this morning, Uncle Joe asked to see me. Once we went back to his office, I knew he'd already heard about you. He asked me about you, so I told him what happened the other night, and about you twisting your ankle. He knows that I like you and that I'm pushing for a relationship. He asked if he could meet you, but I told him it was a little early to be introducing you to the family, and to the madness that comes with that."

"And he still wants to meet me?" Macy sounded surprised.

"Yes, partly because he cares a lot about me, and partly because he's just nosy."

"I'll think about it. Give me your uncle's number." The washing machines stopped, and Bryant transferred the clothes to the dryer as Macy pulled out the items she wanted to air dry.

"You know he will want to meet you in person. He's not really the phone type," he smiled at her. "Hey, why are you pulling out all the fun stuff? I was hoping I would get to fold your underwear," he said jokingly. Macy slapped him on the arm.

"I don't dry my undergarments, but I promise if you're a good boy, I'll let you hang them up in my shower," she said playfully. She enjoyed watching his face light up.

They worked to finish the task at hand, and once again, when it was time to carry everything, Bryant took the brunt of the load. This time she insisted she could walk up the flight of stairs without him carrying her. Tomorrow was Monday, and she would have to go back to work, so she needed to start getting used to using her ankle.

Inside her apartment, he took the laundry baskets to her room and then left her to put her things away while he hung up her undergarments in the bathroom. If that's what made him happy, it was easy enough to let him enjoy himself. She heard him from the other room: "I like this purple number! When do you think I'll get to see you in it?"

Macy laughed, "I still need to go meet your priest first, and you want to know when you can see me wear something that will send you straight into confession. If we do that, I'll never be able to look your uncle in the eye."

Bryant had come into the bedroom to stand by her side. "Now, don't you worry about that. I never go to Uncle Joe for confession. And believe me, there are other things I have to declare because every time I'm with you my thoughts are far from pure." Taking her in his arms, he added, "But I'm in no rush. Even if I have to satisfy myself by replaying our shower scene in my head a hundred times, I want to wait until you're comfortable."

"Only a hundred? Because it plays in my head on a continuous loop," she said as she kissed him.

"You have no idea how much I like the thought of you thinking of me because you haven't left my mind since the moment I met you." He kissed her. It was a soft and gentle caress, nothing crazy or intense. It made Macy realize she wanted something hot and passionate. They stood in her bedroom with the bed just feet away. When she tried to kiss him more deeply her glasses got in the way, so she ripped them off.

"Not tonight, Macy," he said as he drew back. She felt the loss, even though she knew he was right, but it didn't mean she had to like it.

"I have a feeling that I'm going to hate it when you're right." She bit his lip, and he rewarded her with a growl. Taking Bryant's hand, she moved them to her living room, back to the spy equipment. "Now show me what all this stuff does." She shifted some of the boxes to see what he brought her and what she wanted to try first.

For the next hour, Bryant demonstrated how each one of the gadgets worked. Macy had to admit that the new high-tech stuff could make her job easier, but she wasn't sure about the laws regarding planting bugs. Not that she needed to go the legal way to get information—as long as no one found out. Bryant wanted her to know how to work the panic button, not only to scare someone away but also to contact the police if she needed them. She played with the pen's mini recorder, putting it in her purse to see if it would pick up their voices, and testing how far away they had to be before it no longer could hear them. They amused themselves with the night-vision goggles by going into the bathroom and turning out the lights. Then they went out into her apartment where Bryant tried to find her.

They'd had fun that evening doing laundry and acting silly with the gadgets. It had been the strangest date ever, but with Bryant, it didn't really matter what activities they did, because he made everything entertaining, exciting, and always a little frustrating. He would set her body on fire and then cool things down again, over, and over. She had a feeling that once the two of them finally made it to a bed, the building might just burn to the ground. However, at the end of the night, like a gentleman, Bryant tucked her into bed, kissed her goodnight, and locked the door behind him.

They had plans to try out some of the surveillance equipment the next night. Never in her life had she thought she would meet a man like Bryant. He not only wanted to spend time with her, but also, he wanted to help her do her job, and he was genuinely concerned about her safety. She'd been worried about having time for him, but maybe she could have both a career and romance.

After Bryant left Macy's apartment and shut the door behind him, he stood at the closed door, gathering his thoughts. Why had he insisted they not sleep together, when every time she laughed or giggled it put his whole body on edge? The smallest things she did made him want to strip her. He was sure she had no idea how she affected him. Had he really just tucked her into bed and walked out? He could kick himself in the ass. Touching her skin, smelling her hair, drove him mad. The thought of knocking on the door so she would let him back into the apartment, and into her bed, had his feet moving towards the elevator.

Not wanting to go home just yet, he thought he'd stop by the pub and have a drink to relax. But when he walked into O'Shea's Irish Pub and Grill, he knew that going there had been a mistake. His dad, Uncle Joe, and his older brother Mack all sat at a table talking, and the conversation stopped the minute they saw him. Great—they must have been talking about him.

"Just the boy I wanted to see," his dad said. "Come, Bry, sit with us," he pulled out the chair next to him. Bryant didn't see any way to escape what was coming, so he sat and let the fun begin.

"What's this I hear about Friday night?" Mack started in. "Nothing like that ever happens to me when I'm working. I've never had a strange woman come up to me and lay a hot kiss on me," Mack made a kissing sound.

"Just stop that. You're an ass. If you already heard about it, then I don't have anything to add, because you know it all." Bryant didn't want to go into any details.

"Well, I haven't heard what happened," his dad said. Bryant knew his father did already know because most likely that's what the three of them had been talking about when he'd walked through the door.

He turned to his dad, "I find that a little hard to believe when we all know nothing goes on without you knowing. I helped Macy—" they all said at once, "Ahh." He ignored them and continued, "I helped get her out of the pub so that the two guys who were following her didn't know she was gone. I made sure she made it home safely. I like her. End of story."

"Damn right you took her home," his dad said, smiling.

Uncle Joe chimed in, "It seems our little Bryant might have found himself a girl."

"Look, I have to work in the morning. I was hoping to relax with a beer, but I can see I'm not going to get that here." With that, Bryant got up from the table. He heard someone say, "Don't be like that Bry," and then a bunch of laughter from his family as he headed for the door. It sucked having a big family full of intrusive busybodies. As much as he loved them, he disliked them at times, too.

Bryant got in his truck, and on his ride home, his mind filled with thoughts of his night with Macy. They did simple things like her laundry, but that gave them time to talk. Then they played with the stuff he had brought her, and they had fun finding each other with the night vision goggles. It seemed so silly, but this date with Macy was better than any he could remember in a long time. Most dates he had were a bunch of small-talk, a movie to take up time and then a promise to call one another. Being with Macy was so different because he couldn't wait to be with her again and when she talked, he found himself listening to every word and watching her every move.

The next morning, Macy hobbled into work and sat in her small cubicle to go over her notes from the weekend. She was always one of the first to arrive because she liked the office when it was quiet. Once everyone else trickled into the office, she couldn't hear herself think. Her cubicle was so tiny she could barely fit her chair under the desk. With so many people moving around the office during the day it only made her space feel even smaller. Her workstation was the same as everyone else's—three gray-carpeted walls. Her fellow employee's cubicles had pictures of kids playing a sport or performing in a dance recital. Macy's didn't have any personal touches. Two of the walls she filled with documents and papers she didn't want to lose. Sticky notes clung to the edges of her computer screen. If anyone walked by and glanced in her cubicle, they would have thought her a very disorganized person, but Macy had a system that worked for her. No passerby could truly get a good look at her work.

The newsroom started to fill with co-workers who pretended to care about what the others did over the weekend, or asked how their families were doing, but those same people would snatch the story you're working on out from under you in a heartbeat. There were a few Macy considered friends, like the gossip columnist Mindy Love—not her real name. Mindy was a tall blonde bombshell, a little ditzy at times, but she made it work for her. Mindy didn't let many people know how smart she truly was. She said that was how she got people to tell her things that they wouldn't tell someone else. "Play the part," Mindy always said, "and when they think you don't understand, they'll explain it to you." That's how she always got the scoop.

Then there was Dear Judy, the older woman who handed out advice. The picture she had printed next to her column each day was at least thirty years old. Judy was funny, and she always gave honest advice. Some didn't like her tell-it-how-it-is style, but if you didn't want to hear what she had to say, why write in asking for it? Neither Mindy Love nor Dear Judy needed to compete for stories the way the other reporters did, so Macy felt sure the women hadn't befriended her just to get to her story. Not that Macy went out of her way to share her life with them—considering one of them gossiped for a living, and the other gave out advice.

The five cubicles that surrounded Macy's all contained men, some of them weren't bad, but a few of them she couldn't stand. She disliked Jimmy Henderson most of all. He sat directly behind her, and she could always feel him looking over her shoulder, trying to catch a glimpse of her work. Not only did he give her that unpleasant watchful feeling, but he also made comments to her about her clothes. With all of the sexual harassment laws in place, she couldn't even tell a coworker she liked his tie, yet Jimmy Henderson constantly made little remarks to her with hints of underlying sexual interest. He was an average-looking guy with brown hair and a medium build who wore golf shirts most days. She never looked at him long enough to know what kind of pants he wore, and frankly, she didn't care.

The guy in the cubicle next to Jimmy's, diagonally behind Macy, was Stephen Wolfe. On his own, he wasn't so bad, but when Jimmy and Stephen started talking back and forth over the half-wall that separated their workspaces, it drove her crazy. Stephen was tall and lean with sandy blonde hair. He wore a dress shirt and a tie every day.

A man named Kenny Hughes sat next to her. He kept to himself most of the time, and she didn't pay much attention to him either. Kenny was a dark-skinned man with nice eyes who always dressed well. He was one Macy didn't mind. In front of Kenny was William Van Houten, an older gentleman who liked to talk about his grandkids. He was okay by Macy too. He wore wire-rimmed glasses and didn't have much hair to speak of. Every day he came dressed in a suit with a jacket that covered his protruding belly.

The last man that sat near Macy was Billy Furst. Though he sat directly in front of Macy, he liked to talk to Jimmy behind her, so he spent a lot of his time talking over Macy's head. She'd offered to switch desks with him so he could be closer to his friend, but he said he was too lazy to move his stuff. Moving would have solved two of her problems—Billy and Jimmy talking all the time, and Jimmy sneaking around sifting through the papers in her cubicle, looking for a story to steal. Billy dressed casually and always had a camera ready. He was what they called the "ambulance chaser," and he kept a police radio clipped to his hip. If ever there was a quiet news day, Billy looked for a story on Macy's desk—not that she was assigned any big stories.

Bryant arrived at the work site tired and frustrated. All night he'd been thinking about tucking Macy into her bed and cursing himself for always doing the right thing. He wondered how she'd made it into work with her ankle still bothering her. The thought of picking her up in his truck and taking her to work had passed through his mind, but then he'd thought better of it. He didn't want to come on too strong—not that he wanted her to have to use public transportation either.

His crew was working on an old movie theater. The company that had bought the building originally wanted to tear down the theater and build something new, but because it was a historical site, they'd had to keep the building intact. Bryant was working with an architect who understood the stature of that kind of project.

Today Bryant and his men would be doing demolition, being careful not to damage what they would refurbish and replace once the first part of the renovations was over. This was the dirty part of his job, and they had to take the right precautions when working with old materials, like having the building inspected for asbestos before his guys touched anything.

He wanted to meet with his foreman, to see where they stood with the safety inspections. Coffee in hand, Bryant went in search of his go-to guy and found Mark talking to a city worker. Stepping up to the two men, Bryant overheard the inspector say that all the permits and certificates were good to go. They would start on the ground floor and work their way up. A dumpster was in place outside in the alleyway, with a chute attached to slide debris out of the building's upper floors. However, starting from the bottom that day meant they would have to carry the rubble to the container and throw everything over the edge. He knew they were in for a hard day's work and before the day was over sore muscles. It was going to be a long day, and too many hours before he could see Macy again.

Macy worked at her desk until the office became busy, and then went to her boss's office to tell him where she was going. He was the only one who knew what she was working on—besides Bryant and her cop friend. Stopping at his secretary's desk, she asked, "Hey Kim is he busy?"

The young woman shook her head and nodded for Macy to go in. Macy knocked and waited to hear him tell her to enter. Inside, Mr. Sisco sat at his desk, talking on his phone. He held up one finger, so Macy stood and waited by the door. Once he finished with his conversation, he beckoned her to sit in the chair in front of his huge mahogany desk.

William Sisco was the top honcho at the newspaper, and nothing happened without him knowing about it. He was a short, round man, and looking down at him sitting behind his enormous desk only made him seem even smaller. Most of the time, Macy didn't look directly at him because it made her chuckle, and no way did she want her boss to think she was laughing at him. For the most part, he was an easy-going guy—until you missed a deadline, and then you saw an entirely different side of Mr. Sisco. Macy had yet to see this side of him because for some reason he had a soft spot for her.

"Macy, how's the story coming?" he asked, pulling his thick-framed glass from his face.

"I did some research over the weekend—not that I got much—but I did get to speak to one of the club owners. I'm going to try to get my hands on their surveillance tapes, but I'll have to go through the police." Macy took out her notes, "I spoke to Mr. Jim Smith, but I'm sure that's not his real name. I Googled him and found absolutely nothing."

"You know, young lady, we didn't have Google in my day—you had to do the legwork."

"This is one of the reasons why I'm here. I wanted to tell you I'm going down to research the ownership of these clubs. I tried on the computer over the weekend, but I kept coming up with dead ends. I'll be out of the office for most of the morning, maybe longer. While I'm out, I also want to speak with my police source about the surveillance videos. I might not have any luck, because some of the clubs are out of Boddy's jurisdiction."

"You let me know if I can help. I have friends everywhere in this city," he said. Macy started to get up but William stopped her, saying, "Macy, be careful, what you might be onto could be very dangerous, and I'm not inclined to lose my reporters. Make sure someone knows where you are at all times, okay?"

{8}

As Macy walked out of his office, she thought if he only knew what really went on this weekend. She had gone out asking questions, and no one had known where she was. Then again, who would she tell, her mother? Not likely—her mother would have a cow if she knew what Macy was doing. And there was no way she could involve Mindy Love or Dear Judy. So really, who could she have told? She didn't think her boss wanted to get a phone call every time she made a move. After this weekend, Macy knew who would want to know her whereabouts—Bryant.

She stopped by her desk to grab her purse. As she pulled it from the bottom drawer, a thought came to mind. She took the pen, Bryant gave her the night before and hit the "record" button and placed it in the penholder on her desk. That way, she would know if anyone came snooping around her desk while she was away.

When Macy got onto the elevator, she noticed Jimmy standing in the back. With other people crowded in with them, she didn't worry about him, but as the floors went by, people thinned out. Once the doors opened on the ground floor, Jimmy was right behind her. He stepped up close and said into her ear, "Love the plum dress today, but if you're going to wear boots, they should be skyscraper heels, not flats. Now that would be something to see."

His comment almost made her gag. Turning, she said, "I don't think your statement is appropriate in the workplace."

"Ah, don't be like that. You know I didn't mean anything. But if you were interested in a date..."

Macy turned and walked away as fast as her bum ankle would carry her. She had chosen the flat-heeled boots so she could wrap her ankle without anyone noticing because she didn't want to have to explain what happened. What her ankle was going to look like once she removed the boot? She wasn't sure, but she'd probably have to ice it again after walking on it all day. For now, she needed to do her job and forget her ankle, and Jimmy's comments.

By the end of her long day, Macy was exhausted. She needed to go by the newsroom before going home, but she didn't want to run into Jimmy again. It was late, and she hoped the office would be empty. Well, that might not work in her favor if Jimmy was the only one still there.

When she turned the corner, she saw that the newsroom was quiet, if she could only get in and out without anyone noticing. If Jimmy were still there, at least he wouldn't see her from his cubicle.

When she stepped into her workspace, right away she could see that someone had messed with her stuff. The special pen she'd put in the cup holder was out on her desk.

A voice from somewhere in front of her said, "The two assholes of the office were messing with your stuff just to make you paranoid. I told them I'd tell you it was them." Macy looked over her cubicle's wall to see William still at his desk. The older man didn't play childish games—he was old school.

"Thank you, William. Do you know if they were going through my desk, or just messing with what's on top?" She would find out once she was home and could download the recording from her pen.

"I don't know. I came back from the john, and they were already there. I told them they didn't belong at your desk and they said to mind my own business. That's when I said I'd tell you it was them."

"Why must they play childish games? And why can't they leave me alone?"

"Because you're an easy target and you never retaliate. I bet if you got back at them one good time, they would leave you alone." William got up from his desk and came around the divider. He took something off Billy's desk and put it on Jimmy's desk, and then took a piece of paper off his desk and put it on Billy's desk. Smiling at Macy, he said, "This is not my first rodeo."

"But aren't they going to think I did it and then do something else to get back at me?"

"Nope, because they don't trust each other, and by the time they realize neither one of them took the other one's papers, all this will be forgotten." William went back to his desk. "Macy, hang in there and don't let them get the best of you. Did you know, you worry them?"

"I worry them how?" Taking the pen from her desk and putting it into her purse, she walked to his half-wall.

Willam responded, "Well, it's partly because you're a woman, but also because you're more focused, and you pay attention to details."

"Wow, William, that's nice of you to say." Macy thought about it a second and added, "Wait, you're not playing me?"

William smiled, "Not at all. If I were younger and just coming up in the ranks, I would be worried too, but you see, I'm closer to the end of my career, and I honestly don't give a shit anymore. I have a year and then I retire."

On the way home, Macy had to take two buses and walk a block and a half, but it gave her time to think about what William said. Did Jimmy make comments about what she wore to throw her off? Could it be just a tactic? She was sure of one thing—he was looking over her shoulder for information, not just to make her feel uncomfortable.

When she finally opened the door to her apartment, she dropped her bags to the floor. Walking straight to the couch, she started to pull off her boots. Her ankle was throbbing, and she put her feet over the arm of the sofa and tried to breathe. She still needed to unwrap her ankle so she could get a look at it. From the way it felt, it probably would need ice, but for now, she was relaxing with her feet up. She felt as though she could stay that way for days. But after a few long minutes, she knew she had to get up. She headed straight to the bathroom so she could shower. Macy sat on the commode and started to get undressed, taking the bandage off her ankle first. Sure enough, her ankle now appeared a deep mad purple, almost black. Just the look of it made her gasp. Luckily, the swelling hadn't gotten any worse.

Bryant rushed home, fighting the traffic. Normally he would go to the pub, have a drink, and bullshit with some of the regulars. Tonight, he was dirty, tired, and wanted to get back to the city to see Macy. They'd made plans to scope out the layout of the outside of the clubs, checking the back doors and looking for ways the girls could have been taken out without anyone seeing them. The tension in his body vibrated, and he could feel tight knots in his neck and shoulders. He'd thought of her off and on all day, wondering how she was making out with her ankle. Many times, he'd had to divert his thoughts back to the job. By not paying attention was a good way to get hurt on a work site.

He flew through his shower and barely grabbed a bite to eat before he was out the door again, heading back into the city. The drive into the city didn't have as much traffic, so he could really move. By the time, he parked and jogged to Macy's building he was fighting exhaustion. He climbed the front stairs, pushing the button to her apartment. Nothing—no response, he waited a minute and pushed again calling her name. He got nothing. Bryant closed his eyes because if he had rushed to get there when she wasn't home, he might have to... wait. Her voice came over the speaker, "Hello?"

"Macy, it's me." When the door buzzer sounded, relief resonated through his body. He didn't know what he expected to find once he reached her, but his need for her was strong. On the way up in the elevator, he had to talk himself down and remind himself that he would not maul her, no matter how excited he was to see her. Taking several breaths, he counted to ten when the elevator doors opened, then, walking slowly to her door, and knocked.

Macy opened the door. She was wearing bright pink fluffy pants and a tank top. Her hair was tied back, and she had no makeup on. She didn't look as if she was ready to do any investigating—she looked ready for bed. Bryant understood because that's where he wanted to be too. Looking at her now, he wanted to be in bed with her. When she stepped back to let him into her apartment, he took advantage of their close proximity and kissed her. Man, he wanted to do that all day. The thought of having Macy in his life every day and night was becoming a constant feeling of wanting. He looked forward to their time they spent together because he only saw it getting better.

Macy had a way about her that he found appealing. It wasn't just that she was comfortable in her own skin, but it was her strong will and the ability to stand up for what she thought was right.

Just inside her apartment door, Macy wrapped her arms around this amazingly good-looking man who kept coming back. She didn't understand what he saw in her, but he acted as if he enjoyed her company, and Macy had to admit that she liked having him around.

"You don't look like you're ready to do any spying," Bryant said. "You look like you're ready for bed." His thumb caressed her clean skin.

"Long day," she said. She pulled back to close the door, and he noticed she was limping.

Bryant pointed to her foot, "Ankle still giving you trouble? I was hoping it was starting to feel better. Come, sit and let me look at it." When Macy sat down, Bryant took her ankle and put it in his lap, running his fingers over the bruised skin. "Wow, it still looks pretty bad. Are you sure you don't need to see a doctor?"

Macy touched her ankle, "I think it only looks this bad because I was on my feet most of the day. I wrapped it up and wore boots so no one could see how bad it looks, but by the time I got home, my ankle was throbbing. I was resting with it elevated, to help the blood to dissipate. I haven't even had a chance to put ice on it."

Bryant got up and went to her kitchen, just as he had done the other night. She heard him moving around, but this time she knew what he was doing. He came back into the room with a bag of ice, a towel, and the plastic wrap, and once again, Bryant took care of her. He asked if she'd eaten, and when she shook her head to say no, he pulled out his phone and ordered a pizza.

Once Bryant got Macy settled, with her ankle wrapped and elevated on a pillow, he wanted to know how her day had been. She told him how she went all over the city looking for answers to who owned the nightclubs where the girls had disappeared. She'd even gone to look at tax records, but each time she searched, she came up with different names. She told Bryant it was an endless trail of one holding company after another. The one thing that she had uncovered that day was that some of the clubs were under some of the same corporations' names, at different times. It looked like the clubs always sold to a different one of these holding companies every year or so. She planned to research all the corporations tomorrow.

"Almost seems like they don't want anyone to know they're all owned by the same person. I have a feeling that when I get down to the nitty-gritty, I'm going to find that one person owns all of these clubs."

"So, what do you think is happening to these girls?"

"Well, I have some ideas, but I'm trying not to speculate. I don't want my suspicions to steer me down the wrong road. I don't even know if all of the clubs are connected, except that a girl went missing from each place. Of course, the way Mr. Smith reacted to my questions, and the way he had his guys follow me, all tells me that I'm looking in the right direction. But enough about my job. How was your day?"

"We started working on this old theater today. While my crew spent most of their day removing the old seats, Mark and I started clearing out the items we plan to refurbish. Mark is my foreman and a good friend."

The buzzer went off, and Bryant got up used the intercom, to tell the pizza delivery person he'd be right there. Macy watched as Bryant slipped on his shoes and locked the door behind him. She knew she should get up, and at least get plates and drinks, but instead, she sat there thinking about how just a few days ago she'd thought that having a boyfriend wasn't a good idea. Now, in just one weekend, she couldn't imagine not having him around. They talked as if they'd known one another for years instead of days. He hadn't made any more moves to get into her bed, though she knew they both wanted it, it seemed like he wanted to get to know everything about her before he pushed for more. He was perfect—good-looking, caring, and affectionate—almost too good. That thought dispelled when he knocked at her door.

"Pizza delivery," she heard Bryant say.

They ate pizza while they sat and watched a movie Macy snuggled against Bryant. He held her close, but he didn't try to kiss her. That made her think maybe he was waiting for her to kiss him first.

"Bryant, can I ask you something? I feel a little silly asking this, but, why haven't you made any moves romantically?"

He turned, so he faced her and said, "I know I barged into your life at a time when you weren't looking to get involved with anyone. Then I pushed my way into your shower, and I know that was wrong."

"Are you regretting the shower? Because I thought, it was pretty hot. I might not have liked how you just jumped in, but once you were there, I liked it a lot."

"Macy, I don't want you to think for a minute that I'm regretting any part of us, but I was wrong in how I went about it. I have to keep telling myself to slow down and keep my hands to myself."

"Why?"

"I wanted you to get to know me better, and I didn't want to rush you into anything you weren't ready to do. Don't doubt that I want to be romantically involved with you, because that's not even questionable."

"So, are you waiting for a sign? Or do you want me to make the first move, like in the bar?"

Bryant laughed, "That kiss was definitely a pleasant surprise. I enjoyed your initiative. I've never had a woman kiss me the way you did that night. It sent waves of need through my body, and I'm not ashamed to say, I've never felt it that strong before. I'm afraid it will get so hot that I won't be able to hold back. I didn't think you were up for me pushing you into that."

"How will you know unless you try? I mean, not that I want to jump right into bed with you..." Bryant's brows raised, and she corrected her last statement. "Wait, that didn't come out right. I do want to be with you."

Liking the flush that came across Macy's face as she tried to backtrack, Bryant stopped her words with a kiss. It wasn't long before she was underneath him. As his tongue took the inside of her mouth, his body's natural reaction became apparent. He tried to hold his weight off her, so he didn't crush her, and so she didn't feel his hardness, but when she ran her hands down his back to his butt and pulled him against her, he lost all control. Macy's soft sounds were driving him crazy. He could imagine what she'd sound like when he was buried deep inside her body. Then all of a sudden he wasn't hearing her sounds anymore. Instead, he heard his uncle, Father Joe's voice in his head, and that stopped things cold.

"What's the matter? Why did you stop?"

Bryant sat up and sighed, "My damn uncle."

Macy's confusion was apparent, "Your uncle, what about him?"

Standing to readjust his tight jeans, he said, "I told you he's a priest, right? And that he wanted to talk to me on Sunday?"

"Yes," Macy said, but still she didn't understand what Bryant was trying to say.

"I had just met you Friday night, and by Sunday my uncle already knew most of what happened at the pub. When I saw him after Mass, well, he wanted to remind me about lust and how it can make you feel."

"So, while we were making out you were thinking of your uncle?"

"Hell no, I was thinking about the sounds you made... and how it would be when I'm buried deep..." Bryant eased his hand through his hair as he stepped away from her. Macy started laughing—and not a giggle, a big belly laugh, although Bryant didn't find anything funny about the situation.

"So, what you're saying is that your uncle, the priest, has made you feel guilty about having sex with me." Macy wiped tears from her eyes from laughing so hard.

"Yes, and I don't find anything funny about this. When I'm with you, I don't want him popping into my head."

"Well, why don't we try something? If we both agree there will be no sexual intercourse tonight, would that help? We can kiss and touch, but no more. No more than what we already did in the shower, anyway. Well... maybe a little more."

It was Bryant's turn to laugh because she was trying to split hairs. Foreplay without any finale would just build the lust between them and would make his want for her even stronger. He would still have to go to confession, so he thought to himself, what the hell, why not? Stepping close, he crouched down in front of her and touched her cheek.

"Macy, if I touch you, I know that it will lead to more. You need to be the strong one and put a stop to things. I don't know what's happening to me, because I've always been able to control my urges, but with you, I'm not so sure."

"You're not telling me you're a virgin, are you?"

"No."

"So, what's the problem with me? Why are you having trouble having sex with me?"

"Because, you're different, and it wouldn't be just sex, Macy."

"How am I different? You don't even really know me."

"This is going to sound weird, but I just know. And so did Uncle Joe, the minute we started talking about you."

"Have you ever talked with him about any other women before? I mean, if you've—you know, had sex—then why is it a problem now?"

"It's a problem because you are different and I feel differently. I want more."

This totally baffled Macy. Bryant could have sex with someone he didn't care about, but he couldn't do it with her? How could he feel so much for her in such a short amount of time anyway? What more could he possibly want from her? She knew virtually nothing about him. What was he like when he got mad, or when she wanted something different from what he wanted? It had never been her style to jump into anything with both feet, without testing the waters first. Her common sense told her that it was impossible to have such strong feelings for someone so soon after meeting them, but then, she'd always relied more on instinct than on sense. No warning bells had gone off when he said he wanted more, so there wasn't a problem with her instincts. The problem was that she didn't understand how he could know how he felt about her.

"What more are you looking for? I mean, how do you know you want more with me?" Macy got up from her couch and limped into the kitchen with the pizza box. Bryant followed her.

"I just know that by 'more' I mean, for starters, is to get to know you better, and for you to know me. I'm looking for a meaningful relationship that's not just about sex—one that will last and turn into forever."

"And you think I'm the one for that, but not for sex?" She had her back to him as she stood by the counter, but then she felt his arm cage her in. He spoke into her ear, "When it happens, it will be about making love, not having sex. I want love, Macy, not just lust."

"Men aren't supposed to want love. They have commitment problems. They're never the ones who are pushing for more."

"If they don't want more then they're with the wrong person. I know what I want. I just don't know what you want out of this relationship."

{9}

Macy turned to face Bryant because what he was saying was crazy. She just met this man, and he was asking what she wanted from this relationship. "I haven't given it any thought, to be truthful. I don't rush into anything without examining and dissecting it to death. Last week, I didn't think I had the time or the energy to give to a relationship, and then you came along, pushing your way in, so, I have no answer for you—not yet anyway."

"Fair enough, but you know where I stand." He kissed her, a soft touch of his lips, "I should go and let you get some sleep. Will I see you tomorrow?"

"What if I don't want to go to sleep? What if I want to kiss you some more?" Macy felt very strange about the role reversal. The way she'd always seen it, the man was the one who pushed for sex, and the woman was the one who put limits on the relationship. Macy wrapped her arms around his neck and lifted her head so she could bite his lip. Shamelessly rubbing her body against him, she teased him until he pressed her to the counter.

"Macy, I need to go now, before I can't," he said softly. Everything in his body wanted to carry her into her bedroom and strip those cute pink fluffy pants from her body. His hands moved to her back, which he thought was the safest place for them.

"Your loss then, I mean, we agreed on no sex, but if you want to run off, that's your choice. I guess... I could work for a few hours before bed instead." She pulled free from him and went into the living room. Taking the pen, that Bryant gave her from her purse. She sat down, turned it on, and plugged it into her computer.

Bryant followed her into the living room. "I'm not running off at all. I think it's best if we don't press our luck. What are you doing?"

"I left this in the cup holder on my desk while I was out of the office. I wanted to see how well it would work, and I wanted to hear what my co-workers said when I went out. I know for sure they touched things on my desk after I left today because when I got back, the pen was out on my desk instead of in the holder. Then William told me that Jimmy and Billy had been messing with my stuff." She downloaded the information from the pen and hit play.

The recording started. "Do you know what she's working on?" It was Billy's voice.

"Who could tell, with this mess she calls a desk." This time it was Jimmy.

Bryant sat next to Macy. He wanted to hear what her coworkers had to say about her. "Who is that?" he asked.

"The first voice is Billy. He sits in front of me. The other one is Jimmy, the man who sits behind me. I can't stand either one of them, they talk to each other over my head while I'm trying to work," but Jimmy's voice interrupted her.

"You know I asked her to dinner today, and I tried to compliment her on that dress she was wearing. She said my comment was inappropriate in the workplace," he said sarcastically. "All I said was..." Macy stopped the recording.

"Why did you do that?" Bryant wanted to hear what the man was about to say.

"I thought you were leaving," Macy said as she started to get up. Bryant stopped her.

"I know what you're doing. You don't want me to hear what he's about to say, do you? Macy, is this guy harassing you? Because I'll have a talk with him."

"Bryant, I don't need or want you to talk to him. It will only make things worse. I try to ignore him. It's just that there aren't many female reporters in my office. Saying stuff like that is just his way to remind me of that fact. He never says anything that could actually be considered sexual harassment."

"I just heard him say that he asked you out today. If you don't want me to hear what else he said, then I think he has done something to make you feel uncomfortable."

"Bryant, I can fight my own battles. I can handle Jimmy, and I can handle Billy too."

"Is that why you don't want me to hear what he said?"

"He said that he liked my dress, but I should have worn boots that have heels instead of flat boots. His tone was inappropriate, so I told him so and walked away. End of story."

Bryant thought there must be more to it, but he didn't want to push her into telling him. He would find out one way or another. There was no way he was going to let some guy harass Macy. He'd start by making his presence known to her office of men. He wanted them to know she had a boyfriend, but he didn't want to go all "caveman" on her, laying claim to her and dragging her off to his cave by her hair. Okay, it was time for him to leave.

"Do you still want to scope out the clubs tomorrow?" He stood and stepped closer to the door.

"Yes, what time will you be here?"

"That depends on what time I get out of work, and then I'll need to run home to take a shower. Sometimes the traffic leaving the city can be pretty bad, but I'll try to take off a little early."

"You could always bring clothes and shower here. That way we can start checking things out while it's still daylight." He saw a little glint in her eye that seemed to challenge him as if she didn't think he could show up early and take another steamy shower without losing it.

"Now, Macy, that isn't a challenge, is it?" He stepped towards her again. "Because you forget that I have eight siblings, and I take challenges very seriously," he pulled her close.

"Well, you know what they say, cleanliness is next to godliness. But if you can't handle the challenge I completely understand."

"You are one wicked woman, Macy Greene, but I will take you up on that challenge." He kissed her—one last hot kiss before he hit the road. On the ride home, he planned to relive every moment of the shower they'd already taken together that weekend.

After Bryant left her apartment, Macy went back to listening to what her coworkers had to say. It wasn't surprising to hear them talk about her as if she was a piece of ass, and not a fellow reporter. She wasn't going to let that bother her because she knew going into the job that she would be up against chauvinistic males. As long as they didn't touch her, she could handle anything they said. She was glad she now had the pen to leave on her desk, so she would know what they touched, and what they said about her.

The next morning started like any other. Macy arrived at her office early to work on a story she'd covered about a new playground for underprivileged children. It was a fluff story, she knew, because she never got the murders or the major crimes assigned to her. She was amazed that Mr. Sisco had let her look into the missing girls when she'd suggested the story to him. Macy wanted to get the human-interest story out of the way so she could work on her real story and showcase her journalism skills. As long as she kept up with the stories her boss handed down, she was free to work on what she wanted on the side.

By the time the newsroom filled, Macy finished the playground story. Since she was trying to keep her other story a secret, she turned her monitor so that Jimmy wouldn't be able to see it from behind her. Going over her notes, she tried to put the story's events in order, starting with the date each girl went missing, along with when they were reported missing. She wanted to see if there was a pattern. Then she looked at where the girls lived and what schools they went to, but so far, there were no connections. She would have to keep looking. Macy was so deep in thought that she didn't see the deliveryman with the bouquet of flowers until he stood at the opening of her cubicle. Was he even in the right place?

"Macy Greene," he said. The thought that the man had delivered to the wrong cubicle disappeared.

"Hum, yes that's me," she said, taking the huge flower arrangement. "Wait a minute and let me get you a tip."

"No ma'am, the tip's been taken care of, have a good day," he said as he walked away.

As Macy stood to look at the flowers, she noticed that everyone in the office was watching her. There was a card in the little holder, tucked in the midst of the white roses in the center. She couldn't imagine who could have sent her flowers, and apparently, no one else in the office could either. Pulling the card free from the envelope, she heard Jimmy ask if it was her birthday from somewhere behind her. She ignored him and read the card to herself, "Dear Macy, hope you're having a great day. I want every man in that office to know that you're taken. Bryant."

Macy started to laugh. Leave it up to Bryant to make his point. She tucked the card into her purse, smiling just a little because she'd never received flowers at work before. Her smile disappeared when Jimmy, who had snuck up behind her, asked her who Bryant was. She looked over her shoulder, and there he was, standing behind her, stretching his neck to see the card.

"Do you mind?" Macy shrugged Jimmy away, "I swear you are so nosy."

"Well, it must be your birthday. I couldn't read the other part of the card, just the guy's name."

"No, it's not my birthday, and Bryant is none of your business."

"Oh, so it must be a boyfriend then. Well, that explains why you wouldn't go out with me. Although I'll admit, I was leaning toward you being a lesbian. Not that I'd have a problem with you bringing a friend with you, if you were, that is, a lesbian, I mean—not the boyfriend."

Macy heard William say from the other side of the divider, "Shut up, you ass."

Bryant's phone chimed with an incoming text message. He pulled it from the side pocket of his cargo pants. The text was confirming the flower delivery he order for Macy this morning. He didn't expect to hear anything from her when she received them, but he hoped that when he finally made it over to her place that night, she would thank him in person. Now he couldn't wait until the end of the day when he would shower at her apartment, and they would go investigating.

The thought of Macy naked in her shower came to mind, and Bryant smiled. He was hoping she would join him, and that he'd be able to touch her without his Uncle's voice in his head. In his mind, he could see her standing naked, with the shower curtain pulled snugly against her body, as if the flimsy curtain could hide her beauty from him. He had imagined her a hundred times since seeing her in the shower that day. Closing his eyes, Bryant relived the moment she'd revealed herself to him. When she'd gone under the water and put her hands to her head to wet her hair, his eyes had taken in her ravishing body, and her full breasts with dark-rose colored, perfectly puckered nipples. He remembered his need to touch her and once again felt he wouldn't have been able to stop. He'd let his eyes roam further down her body, to her thin waist and flat stomach…

"Bryant, you okay?" The voice of his foreman broke Bryant's daydream of Macy. Shit, he was standing around fantasizing on the job. Thank God, he'd worn loose pants today.

"Yeah, what's up? I was just thinking," he said—not that he would elaborate on what he was thinking, or who was in his thoughts.

"I don't think I've ever seen you as distracted as I have the last couple of days. Is everything okay with your family? They're the only ones I can think of who could take your mind off work like this. You're usually focused," Mark said, sounding confused.

"I met someone, and she's on my mind," Bryant said flatly. He didn't want to go into detail.

Mark asked, "That chick from Friday night at the pub?" How did Mark know about that? Bryant shouldn't have been surprised, because he knew that every member of his family had a big mouth. Mark sometimes went to the pub after work, before going home to his wife and kids. He was friends with Bryant's older brother Mack, and the two of them gossiped like women.

"I swear. Don't you and Mack have anything better to talk about besides my life? How sad," Bryant shook his head and got back to work.

"Look, Bry, when a strange lady kisses you like she did, smack in the middle of a bunch of people who know you, what do you expect? Of course, people are going to talk."

"Whatever, let's just get back to work so I can get out of here sometime today."

"I heard she was hot as hell," Mark said. When Bryant turned and gave him a stern look, he rephrased, "I mean she was pretty."

Bryant wasn't going to talk to Mark about Macy, even if he did consider him a friend because what was going on between the two of them was nobody's business. Besides, he wanted to have her all to himself for a little while longer. Once his mother heard about Macy, she'd want her to come to church and Sunday dinner with the entire family. Even if more than half of the family already knew about her existence, he didn't want to overwhelm Macy or scare her off by bringing her to dinner too soon.

Macy had said she'd been an only child, so Bryant knew that meeting a big family like the O'Shea's would definitely be an overwhelming experience for her. Knowing he had eight siblings, and sitting at a table with them, was two different things. Besides, it wasn't just family at Sunday dinner—his mother would invite anyone who was hungry or down on their luck. There were times when Bryant himself didn't even want to be there. His family dinners could become crazy and loud pretty quickly. When that happened, Bryant liked to go outside to the old fort they'd built when they were kids. There he could have some peace and quiet—until someone realized he was missing and sent Ray out to get him.

Bryant knew Macy would have to meet his family if she hung around long enough, but the longer he could put it off, the better. Someday, Macy would get comfortable with his crazy family, but it had only been days since they'd met. Bryant wanted her to be relaxed around him first and him around her before they brought other people into it. He wanted time to learn her ways. He'd already seen her mad, and scared, but he wanted to learn what made her happy and what made her feel good. The thought of pleasing her brought his mind back to her body, and the little sounds she made when they kissed. He could only imagine what she would sound like in bed, and he wanted to find that out more than anything.

Riding the bus home while holding the flowers Bryant had sent her wasn't easy, but Macy did her best to keep them out of her neighbors' faces. The arrangement was beautiful, and there was no way she would leave it at work. She wanted to put them on her table, where she could admire them every day. Their fragrance was wonderful too, although the woman in the seat behind her kept sneezing.

Macy loved the fact that Bryant was thinking about her. She was thinking about him, too. In fact, he was on her mind a lot. Although she knew she needed to talk to Bryant about his display of ownership of her. She did think the roses could potentially stop the harassment that Jimmy liked to do to her when he made comments about her clothing. Now that he knew she had someone in her life, he might lose interest in her. She would still be a woman in the newsroom—that wasn't going to change—but maybe now that men in her office knew she was taken, they would just ignore her. That would be a relief.

When the bus came to Macy's stop, she moved to the front to get off. As she walked down the aisle, she heard people saying things like, "Oh, thank God she's getting off." Making her way off the bus wasn't easy. With the flowers in her face, she couldn't see the steps and certainly didn't want to fall when her ankle was starting to feel better. Once she was safely on the sidewalk, she smiled and waved to her fellow riders. One of the other passengers gave her a one-finger wave—the middle finger.

Macy had to walk the rest of the way home. Her mind was on what was going to happen once Bryant made it to her apartment. Although it would serve him right to let him shower by himself, although that would also deprive her.

As she approached her building, she noticed a large man standing on the front stoop. She realized it was one of the men who had followed her Friday night. Putting the flowers in front of her face, she walked right past her building, thinking, *oh crap, oh crap, now what am I going to do? They know where I live, and I can't get into my apartment.*

Walking around to the back entry, hoping she could get in that way, Macy held her breath as she turned the corner. Right away, she spotted the other man from Friday night, guarding the back door. She wasn't going to press her luck—she hurried away in the opposite direction.

She shifted the flowers so she could pull out her phone. She needed to call Bryant. As his phone rang, she stepped into a coffee shop.

"Hey, Macy, I'm on my way now," he said happily, "and I've been looking forward to this all day."

"Well, I have some bad news for you. I'm not at the apartment, because the two goons from the other night are guarding the front and back doors."

"Where are you now?" His tone had changed to concern, she could hear it in his voice.

"I'm in the coffee shop just around the corner from my building, The Steaming Mug."

"Good, stay there. I'll be there in like two minutes." He was further away than that, but he'd still make in two minutes time.

"Like I plan to go anywhere," she said sarcastically. "Can't you can get them to go away? I need to get inside my apartment."

"Macy, they know where you live now. Even if I could get them to leave, they'll be back. You can't stay there for now. It's not safe."

Macy pulled the phone away from her ear and stared at it almost as if looking at it would change something. She couldn't believe what he was saying. "Bryant, I have to stay there. I live there." She said the words very slowly so he would understand.

"Just wait for me, okay?"

As she disconnected the call, she had a feeling that she wasn't going to like what Bryant had to say. Macy went to the counter to order her favorite mocha latte. She decided she needed the caffeine, even if it would keep her up all night—not that she would be getting much sleep anyway after this scare. She grabbed a table where she could see the door and waited for Bryant.

Bryant pulled into a spot that was further away from the coffee shop than he would have liked, but he wanted to walk past Macy's building so he could get a good look at the guy. As he started walking, he called Fred, the retired cop, who tended bar at the pub during the day. He should be just getting off work. If things escalated, maybe he could call one of his fellow officers to help. Bryant heard, "O'Shea's," Fred murmured in his deep voice.

"Fred, this is Bryant. I need a favor. Two goons are standing in front of Ma—in front of a friend's place, and I was hoping you could call a friend to help them to move it along. One is standing out front, and one is in back. They're waiting for someone to let them into the building, and I really don't want them inside. You could say someone called in and reported two suspicious characters. And if I could get info on them, you know names and addresses that would be great." He gave Fred Macy's address.

"Is this for the lady that kissed you Friday night? Heard all about that," Fred laughed.

"Man, what is up with everyone? You'd think nothing exciting ever happens around here. When did everyone turn into a bunch of gossiping women?"

"I've worked here for years and years, and no strange lady has ever walked up and laid one on me. So, I guess when something like that happens to the guy that only works here one or two days a week, people start to talk."

Bryant laughed. "Fred, your wife would kill you if she found out some strange woman kissed you, so just look at it this way—I saved your life." Bryant was close enough to Macy's building to see the huge man standing on the stoop talking to an old lady and trying to convince her to let him into the building. "Hurry, Fred, the guy is pushing an old lady around trying to get in," Bryant warned. The line went dead. Fred was already calling his police friends.

{10}

Bryant saw the old lady hit the goon with her umbrella and shut the door behind her. He could hear her yelling about how she was going to call the cops. Bryant thought, perfect. Now I don't have to save a little old lady today, and if she calls the cops along with Fred's call, then there will be two complaints.

He walked past as the big man banged on the door and yelled back at the older woman. Now he just had to figure out what he was going to do with Macy because she definitely would not be staying here. He knew where she could stay, but would she agree with his suggestion?

As he approached the coffee shop, he was trying to think of a way to convince her to go along with his proposal. While his idea had its own dangers, and even though it wouldn't be easy on him, Macy's safety was the most important thing.

Opening the door to the coffee shop, Bryant looked for Macy but didn't see her. Then he realized the bouquet of flowers sitting on one of the tables was blocking someone from view, and he knew it had to be her. He stepped up to her table just as she was bringing her drink away from her lips. A little bit of white foam stuck to her upper lip, and Bryant almost died when her tongue came out to lick it off. As he stood watching her, his mind went to some unholy places. When her eyes finally reached his, she looked confused by his reaction.

Bryant crouched so he was eye level with her. She was wearing her dark-rimmed glasses, and her long brown hair was free, hanging to the top of her breasts. He wanted to wrap his fingers in her hair and pull her towards him.

"Hey, you okay?" He saw her release a deep breath, and then she nodded.

"What am I going to do, Bryant? I've been sitting here thinking— where I can go? I guess... I could stay with my parents." He didn't want her to do that.

"No, I mean, if they found your apartment then they could find your parents' house too, and you don't want to get them involved in this mess." He knew her staying with him was the safest place for her.

"No, I guess not. But I can't afford to stay in a hotel indefinitely until I figure out what's going on." She bit her lip, worrying about what she was going to do.

"Come and stay with me, Macy." He watched as the shock crossed her face and he knew right then that she was going to refuse. To stop her from saying no, he quickly said, "Look, I don't know what these guys want with you, but think about what you're investigating. Missing girls, Macy, and I don't think it's such a stretch of the imagination to think they won't just grab you too. Walking by your building just now, I watched one of the guys try to push around one of your elderly neighbors, trying to get into the front door. What's going to happen, Macy, once they make it inside?" Bryant wanted her to think about what might transpire if she insisted on staying at her apartment.

"Oh my God, did they hurt anyone? This situation is entirely my fault." Macy started to fret.

Bryant told her, "Only the goon got hurt because, the older lady hit him with her umbrella and went inside, yelling something about calling the cops,"

"Oh, that must have been Mrs. Wilkins. She always carries an umbrella, even on sunny days." Macy released a sigh because this was starting to get out of hand.

"Macy, my point is that if they are willing to harass your neighbors to get into your building, what's going to happen once they are inside? I doubt they plan to knock on your door to say hello. I have a feeling they're not only looking for you but for what you might have found out about the missing girls." Macy's eyes got big.

"Bryant, my computer! It has my notes and everything else I've found out. I have to get back into my apartment to get my stuff—before they ransack it." Now she saw his point, but there was no way he was letting her anywhere near the building.

"Macy listen, you can't go back into your apartment." When she started to protest, "I have…," he stopped her with a kiss. "Listen, I will go and get your stuff because they aren't looking for me. I can slip in and out of the building without them even looking my way. Just give me your keys and then once I'm in, I'll call you, and you can tell me what you need me to grab. You can stay safely here, and I'll pick you up the moment I'm done." He was worried she was going to fight him on the fact that she could not go back into her apartment.

Macy retrieved her keys and handed them over. He was right—she'd never have been able to get into the building. While he was gone, she would have to think of somewhere else she could stay, because she definitely wouldn't be staying with Bryant.

After he left, her mind drifted to the things she was going to need once he made it inside. She closed her eyes and thought about how he was going to be getting very personal with her private things. Thinking about him going through her undergarments and touching everything made Macy's face flush.

It was taking him a long time to call her. After all, her building was just around the corner. She hoped that he hadn't run into any trouble. Behind her bouquet of flowers, Macy stared hard at her cell phone, willing it to ring. When it did, it scared her. She snatched her phone off the table and hit answer.

By the time Bryant made it back to Macy's building, there was already a police car parked out front, but he didn't see anyone on the stoop. Either the goons had left on their own, or the cops had already taken care of them. For all he knew, the men could be waiting right across the street and watching the door. Unlocking the outer door, Bryant looked behind him. He didn't see anybody, so he went inside and walked to the elevators. That was where he spotted two cops, and they were walking the two big guys out of the building. Now Bryant was hoping the police got to the men before they could break into Macy's apartment.

He was happy when he found her door still intact. When he put the key into her door, he felt almost as if he was the one who was breaking in. Once inside, he dialed Macy. He knew he'd have to gather everything she might need, at least for that night, if not for the week, or longer. He didn't see this situation clearing up anytime soon, and as long as Macy was in any danger, she couldn't come back here.

She sounded out of breath as she said hello. "Hi, Macy, I'm in now. So where do you want me to start?" He looked around her apartment, waiting for her to tell him where to go.

"Okay, first, go to my office and grab my computer. I have my satchel next to my desk. In the top right drawer, there is a folder, I'd like you to grab it, and in the bottom drawer, is all the stuff you bought me at the spy store. I want all of that. And if it won't fit in the satchel, then I have a backpack in the closet." Macy let out a frustrating breath as she listened to Bryant move through her apartment.

"Okay, what's next?" He already knew where she was going to send him next.

"Now go to my bedroom. I need clothes for work until I can get back into my apartment. Start with my closet. I have my work clothes on the right. There are a few dresses and some pants—grab those. On the floor are my shoes. I'm going to need at least five or six pairs." She was picturing her closet and how she had her clothes set up.

"Damn, Macy, you have so many shoes, which ones do you want me to take?" Bryant looked down at about fifty pairs of shoes and had no idea which ones he should bring.

"Take one of each of the main colors. You know—black, brown, navy. But make sure they are either flats or low heels." She closed her eyes thinking about if she had any special shoes she wanted him to bring.

They went over some more things in her bedroom, but when it came for him to pick out bras and underwear for her, he knew that if he looked at each one, it would send him over the edge. He thought about the time when he hung up the few bras in the shower for her, but now he was touching all of her private stuff. Instead of choosing items one by one, he closed his eyes and counted. Once he knew he had enough, he then grabbed a bunch more. He put the clothes into the backpack and set the packed bags by the door. Then he when into her bathroom, grabbing her toothbrush, shampoo, and anything else he could think of throwing into the bag.

Before he left, he went back to her office and took a piece of tape from her desk. He planned to put it on the bottom of her door and doorjamb. That way when he came back, he could see if the tape had been disturbed, and he would know if anyone had entered her apartment. Once outside, he knocked on her neighbor's door. The old lady who'd fought the man with her umbrella earlier opened the door, and Bryant smiled at the older woman standing in front of him.

"I'm sorry to bother you, but I'm a friend of your neighbor, Macy Greene."

He was surprised when she said, "I know."

"Can I ask a favor? You know the men that were by the front door earlier? If you happen to see them again, will you call the police right away?" Bryant asked, "It's Mrs. Wilkins, right? Macy has told me so much about you." The older woman smiled. She couldn't have been more than five feet tall, and about seventy-five or eighty years old, but she looked pretty damn tough. With her gray hair and round body, she could have been his grandma.

"Oh, I plan on it. If those guys think they can push this old lady around then, they have another thing coming. I don't take any shit from thugs, and believe me. I know everything that happens in this hallway." She gave him a cheeky smile as if she knew things.

Bryant worried that if the men did get into the building again, the woman might try to confront them herself. And he did think they would be back. "Mrs. Wilkins, please, if you see them don't try to stop them, just call the cops, okay? I wouldn't want to see you get hurt, and I'm sure Macy would feel awful if anything happened to you." The mention of Macy's name seemed to soften the woman's facial expression. "Now, I don't want you to worry about Macy," he continued. "She's going to stay with me for a few days, so no one should be going in or out of her apartment—nobody except for her or I, alright, Mrs. Wilkins?" Bryant hoped she wouldn't get caught up in this mess and get hurt.

The little old lady nodded and smiled up at him.

Bryant took Macy's things to his truck then went to pick her up from the coffee shop. Once she and her flowers were safely inside, he headed out of the city, towards his place. She was very quiet, and in a way, it unnerved him. Not knowing what she was thinking drove him crazy.

"Macy, what are you thinking? You're not worried about staying at my place, are you?" He glanced over at her and then his eyes when back to the road.

She looked straight ahead and said into the air, "I'm not staying with you. I have a few friends I could stay with."

"What do you mean you're not staying with me? Because that's where we're going. It's the safest place for you. I can take you back and forth to work every day. I don't mind. I don't think you should get anyone else involved. What if the goons find your friends?" He tried to look at her, but he was driving and didn't want to get into an accident while trying to keep her safe.

"I don't think I should have gotten you involved, and yet here we are. Bryant, you can't seriously think me staying with you is a good idea. You can't even touch me, much less be confined in a small space with me day in and day out. It's definitely not going to be good for me. I already feel frustrated every time you're at my place, and you stop things from going all the way." She looked out the side window so he couldn't see her face.

Bryant started laughing. She didn't want to stay with him because she was sexually frustrated. Well, she could join the club, because being with her was all he'd been thinking about ever since the moment she kissed him. He wanted to get her naked and under him. Hell, even her licking that white foam from her lip at the coffee house had him fantasizing about her. He looked over at her, but she didn't seem happy with him. He pulled both of his lips in and bit them together as if holding back a laugh because it was funny, both of them being so frustrated.

Macy huffed, "Oh, you think that's funny, do you? Just wait, and I can guarantee that you won't be laughing for long after I get done with you, Bryant O'Shea."

"Does that mean you're staying with me, Macy Greene? Because I look forward to it, and you're not the only one who is frustrated. Believe me, when I saw you licked that cream off your lip earlier, well, dammit woman, you nearly killed me." Once again, he glanced over at her to see her reaction.

Now it was her turn to laugh, "Is that why you were looking at me so intensely? Well, at least I know it's mutual. If you force me to stay with you, even if it's for my safety, well then, I plan to take full advantage of the time we spend together." She folded her hands in her lap because she didn't know what to do with them. If she were only braver, she'd put a hand on his thigh.

They drove out of the city and over the bridge. It was only going to take them ten more minutes to reach his house. He shifted in his seat because he realized for the first time that, since he had no idea she would be coming over, his house was a mess. Not only, were there dishes in the sink and clothes tossed about, but there was wood piled in the living room because he was also in the process of renovating the house. There's only one bedroom finished—not that he minded sharing it with her, but if she wanted her own space, then he would have to clear out some construction materials. She could always use his room, and he could sleep on the couch. Maybe he should warn her about the mess before they got there.

"Macy, I think I told you how I'm working on my house. Well, before we get there, I wanted to let you know what to expect. It's a mess. If I'd known you were coming over, I would have cleaned up a bit. I'm trying to work on one room at a time, starting with what's most important." He glanced over at her to see her reaction. She didn't appear affected at all.

Well, he thought, here we go. Bryant pulled into his driveway and turned off his truck. It was already dark outside so she wouldn't see the full effect of the house. He turned to Macy and watched as she looked out the windshield at the old Victorian, built in the eighteen hundred's, with a wraparound porch supported by huge pillars. He knew it looked rough on the outside, but only because he hadn't gotten around to fixing it yet.

"Oh Bryant, it's beautiful. I just love this style house." She jumped out of the truck and walked up the small path that led to the front steps. After hopping up the stairs on her good ankle, she walked the length of the porch, turning around in the attached gazebo at the end. He enjoyed watching her. It was almost as if he could hear her mind turning.

"Bryant, I see a beautiful table here, and benches all around, and a family having dinner out here in the summer. Oh, and a porch swing over here, and rockers in front, oh and big flower pots over here," she pointed. Even in the evening light, he could see the glint in her eyes. "I can't wait to see the inside. You have to show me everything."

He unlocked the door and Macy went in first. "Wait here a minute, and I'll turn on lights," he told her. He stepped away from her, and then within seconds light filled the room. Bryant couldn't take his eyes off her as she looked around and took in the living room. She didn't seem to notice the mess and looked at the room itself. Macy gazed at the high ceilings, walked to the fireplace, and ran her hand over the mantle. He could imagine pictures of her sitting up there, and he thought she imagined that too.

She moved into the next room, a formal dining room. Bryant hadn't done a thing to improve it. The room still had its old wallpaper, which was peeling halfway down the walls. Macy ran her hand over the chair rail that bordered the room at waist height. She looked overhead at the chandelier, then down to the floors, but she didn't say a word.

When she was ready, Macy moved to the next room. The kitchen still had the original cabinets, but it held new appliances. He hadn't had a chance to sand down the hardwood floors yet either. He moved to stand in front of the sink, hoping she wouldn't see the mess he had in there. She wasn't looking at his dirty dishes, though. She was still just taking everything in, her eyes scanning the entire room.

"Macy, you haven't said a word since we came inside. What are you thinking?"

"I'm not talking because every room I go into, I see colors and patterns on the walls. I see furniture in all the rooms. Then I realize that this is not my house to decorate. I know it still needs a lot of TLC, but the potential is overwhelming." She turned to face him, "I absolutely love it so far. Show me more, please?"

He took her hand and walked with her into the den, and then he showed her the sunroom off the back of the house. Next, he took her up a flight of stairs to the second floor. This floor had four bedrooms, along with two bathrooms. Avoiding his bedroom and its mess, he guided her up the next set of stairs. This level held several rooms, meant to be extra bedrooms or playrooms for children and a bathroom.

Finally, the only places he hadn't shown her were the basement and his room. He couldn't put off showing her the rest any longer. Taking her hand, he led her back down to the second floor.

Bryant stood at his closed bedroom door and said, "This is my room, and it's finished, but it's a mess. If you give me a few minutes, I'll clean up, and then you can come in. Alright?"

"Okay, I'll wait right here," she said, and he disappeared into the darkness of the bedroom and shut the door.

Bryant ran around the room picking up clothes and throwing them into the bottom of his closet, and then he went into his bathroom to clean the mess in there. Coming back into his room, he quickly made his bed, wishing he had more time to change his sheets. When he opened the door, Macy was standing near the stairs with her hand moving up and down the wood of the banister. He liked to see her feel the wood because he knew how he felt when he did the same thing. He wondered what she thought as she did it.

He asked as she walked back to his side. "When you run your hand over the wood like that, what are you thinking?"

"I don't know," she said. "Maybe I can see how it will look. I can see a beautiful handrail, soft and smooth, with a glossy finish on it."

"You know that's what I do for a living—bring old buildings back to their former glory. I see things for what they can be again." Taking her in his arms, he leaned down to kiss her. When their lips touched, it sent a sensation throughout his body. He slowly walked them back toward his bedroom.

Scooping her up in his arms, he said, "Time to get clean so we can get dirty because I plan to relieve some of that pent-up sexual tension you have." The sound she made had his body going hard. "You okay with that?"

"Yes, please," her words came out as a moan that made him start undressing her right away.

"I need to touch you, Macy. God knows I've tried to be good. You do things to me that make my heart throb and ache for you." He took her glasses off and set them on the sink, then slowly unbuttoned her top. "When I look at you, I see how things could be between us." Sliding her top off her shoulders, he said, "You're beautiful, Macy."

Kissing her bare shoulder, he felt her skin with his lips, running his tongue over her, tasting her. Macy's head dropped back, and he could feel her chest rising and falling as if she was trying to get enough air to breathe. He moved his mouth down her chest, kissing the swells of her breasts as his hand caressed her through her bra. Working his way down her body with his mouth, he went down on his knees so he could kiss her flat stomach. He undid the button and zipper on her slacks, sliding them down her thighs. He slipped her shoes off and flung them away.

On his way back up her body, his rough hands glided up the back of her smooth legs as he kissed his way up. When he reached her sweet spot, he couldn't help taking in her scent. He felt her body quiver, and he thought *Jesus, Mary, and Joseph, I want her.* She pulled him to his feet.

"Now your turn," she said. Bryant knew he would never make it once she touched him.

{11}

Bryant tried to stop Macy from taking off his clothes. He knew how they smelt from working all day, but he couldn't discourage her. "Macy honey, it might be best if I do my own clothes because if you start for me, I might embarrass myself." She chuckled, but she didn't stop. She started to remove his work shirt. "Macy, seriously," he said, as he tried putting his hands over hers to stop her movements. She laughed again and slapped his hands away.

"No way, are you backing out this time," she said. Once she'd gotten his shirt unbuttoned, she yanked it down over his arms and helped it fall to the floor. Then she grabbed the hem of his t-shirt, and off it went over his head. "I stood still while you touched me. You think that was easy for me?" When she went to her knees to undo his pants, Bryant had to close his eyes against some of his earlier thoughts that suddenly came back. She untied his work boots, and immediately his thoughts went to how his feet would smell once she pulled them off because having his feet in the boots day-in and day-out didn't make for a very pleasant fragrance.

"I'll get them," he said, stopping her. "They're hard to get off, and besides, you might not want to be too close to me when they come off—if you know what I mean." He toed them off and kicked the boots to the other side of the small bathroom. Macy stood looking into his eyes as she undid his cargo pants. He was so hard. He wouldn't even need a hammer to drive in nails just then. After she let his pants fall to the floor, they were both standing in just their underwear. He couldn't wait any longer. He wrapped his hands around her and drew her in for a kiss. As their mouths met, Macy's hands slid up and down his back. The sensation made his skin prickle with goosebumps, and he shivered under her touch.

He unclasped her bra and skimmed the strap down her arms. Just two more articles of clothing and they would be completely naked, together again.

"I need to start the water. It takes a while to warm up."

While he was turning the water on, Macy removed the last barrier so that when he turned back to her, he almost lost it. There she stood his eyes free to roam over her body. She looked exquisite, with her petite frame and delicate features. "Macy, do you have any idea just how beautiful you are? I could look at you forever and never get tired of seeing you."

He could tell that in spite of her bold behavior, she was still a little uncomfortable, so he said, "The water should be ready let's get in." When she stepped behind the curtain, he gave himself a second to gather his thoughts before taking off the last thing that kept him sane. It wasn't as if they hadn't been in the same predicament once before, but last time he hadn't given any thought to it. This time he couldn't think about anything else.

"You coming in or chickening out?" Macy called. Oh yes, he was definitely getting in with her.

When Macy felt Bryant's hard body press against her back, she couldn't stop the smile that crossed her face. His hands came around and caressed her abdomen, and his hardness tucked into the cleft of her butt. She took his hands in hers and moved them up to her breasts, to show him how she liked to be touched.

"Oh God, Macy, I want you so badly," he said as he kissed the side of her neck. His hands took over, and she was free to feel his body. Her reach was limited because he stood behind her, but she managed to slide her hand between them and take his stiffness. Macy worked her hands up and down as she listened to his groans. She knew when he pushed into her hand that he was close.

"Macy you're going to make me come if you keep that up," he moaned. "I prefer for that to happen when I'm inside of you."

"I thought we were just relieving some of that pent-up sexual tension we talked about earlier?" She giggled until he skimmed one hand down through her pubic hair. Bryant had one hand still on her breast while the other spread her to find her sensitive spot, making Macy moan. This was what she needed. His touch made her hold him tighter. When Bryant bit down on her shoulder, they both came.

As they caught their breath again, Bryant held her, tucking her in tight against his body. He said into her ear, "The next time, I want to be inside you when I watch you come." Then he kissed her as if his life depended on it.

This time when they washed each other, Bryant didn't miss a single spot on Macy's body. As they dried off, he asked, "Are you hungry, because I'm starving." He wrapped a towel around his waist and turned to look at her.

The sight of him made Macy wonder how she'd gotten so lucky. When they'd joked about the day they met and how it was her lucky day, she had no idea how true that really was. This perfect specimen of a man was all hers—the man she hadn't been looking for, found her. Bryant pulled on a pair of boxers and handed her one of his t-shirts.

"Just wear this for now," he said, "because your bags are still in my truck. I'll get them after we have something to eat."

Macy reminded him, "Don't forget to grab my flowers. Now let's eat." After her trying day, Bryant's helpful rescue, and their steamy shower, Macy was ready for dinner, and bed.

Bryant went downstairs to find something for them to eat, giving Macy a few minutes to think. She walked around his room, looking for personal touches. He had a big fireplace in his room, with a few pictures of his family on the mantle. She picked them up one at a time and examined them, first looking for him, and then examining everyone else. In the first photo, his father looked like a tough man, but then again, if she'd had nine kids to raise, Macy guessed she would have been tough too. Then there was Bryant's mother, the woman had a stern look on her face, but she had her arms around three of the kids.

In the next picture, everyone was smiling. Looking at each member of his family, Macy could see how they looked the same, but different. Each one had red hair but in different shades. Some appeared to be more brownish-red, and others had blondish-red hair. One guy had a red beard and blond hair, and that made her smile. She placed the photos back where he'd had them and moved to the side of his bed. It wasn't a big massive bed, and it didn't have any fancy comforter or pillows on it. From where she stood, she turned to look out the double windows, down into the dark yard below.

Suddenly a light came on, and she watched as Bryant walked out in his boxers and lit the grill. An overwhelming feeling came over her as she watched him. She wanted him. The house he'd chosen for himself—she could see a big family living there. Did she want a big family? Just then, she imagined a few kids playing in the yard on a swing set built by their father.

Shaking her head, Macy snapped out of her dreamland. Thinking like that was crazy. They'd just met a few days ago, and already she was picturing them married, with a few kids running around. She walked away from the window and went downstairs to see if Bryant needed any help. She found him washing dishes.

"Hey, sorry again that my place was such a mess, if I'd known you were coming I swear I would have cleaned up first."

"Don't worry about that. I truly think your place is charming." Macy took a dishcloth in hand and started drying the dishes he'd just washed. Bryant looked over at her. "You know you don't have to do that."

"I know, but I think that if I'm going to stay here, then I should earn my keep."

"No, you don't. I asked you to stay as a guest, not a maid."

"Oh, that's funny. I don't quite remember you asking me to stay here at all. If I recall correctly, you demanded that I stay here," Macy said with a grin. "Don't worry helping you will make me feel better because I don't want to be a total moocher." She started opening cabinets so she could put the dried dishes away. Since they were mostly empty, it wasn't hard for her to find places to put things.

"Let me go check on the grill—I put steaks on. I'll be right back."

Macy continued doing the dishes when suddenly she heard footsteps approaching. A man yelled from the direction of the front door, "Bryant, it's just me. I smell steak cooking. Hope you have enough for two…" his words stopped when he caught sight of Macy standing at Bryant's sink, doing dishes wearing only Bryant's t-shirt, and nothing else.

Just then, Bryant walked through the back door. He looked at his brother, then back to Macy. It was Patrick, one of the twins. At only twenty years old, it was possible Patrick had never seen anything like Macy Greene before.

Shit, Bryant thought, *I know he can see right through that damn t-shirt.* He stepped in front of Macy to block his brother's view.

"Patrick, what are you doing here? Have you ever heard of calling first?"

"I never call. But then again, I've never found beautiful almost-naked women doing your dishes before either. Maybe I should stop by more often." Patrick attempted to step around Bryant to introduce himself to Macy, who was tugging at the hem of the t-shirt.

"Not a chance," Bryant said, blocking his brother again. "Macy, please go back upstairs until I get rid of my brother." He felt her snuggle into his back, and he moved when she did, so he continuously blocked her from Patrick's view. When she made it to the doorway, Macy turned and made a run for it, and again Bryant stood in the way.

Bryant put two potatoes in the microwave then turned to his brother. "So, what are you doing here? And when are you leaving?"

"You are going to put some pants on so we can talk," Patrick said, sitting down at Bryant's table.

"No, I'm not, because you're not staying."

"Is that the girl from Friday night? Man, I heard she was hot, but…" His words trailed off when he saw his brother's face.

"That's none of your business. And don't go blabbing about what you saw here tonight, or so help me God, Patrick, I will be going to hell, for murder. Do you understand?"

Patrick put up his hands defensively. "Hey, you know you can't hide anything for long without Mom catching wind of it, and once that happens, all hell will break loose anyway."

Bryant heard Macy coming back down the stairs. He turned to see that she was back in her work clothes, *Dammit*, this was not at all how he had seen their night going.

"Bryant, look, I don't think it's a good idea for me to stay here. Maybe you could take me to my friend's place after all."

"She's living here too? Oh, shit. Mom is going to have a cow when she finds out. You know you're going to have to marry her, right?" Bryant put his hand over his younger brother's big blabbing mouth.

He said to her, "No, Macy, you're staying." He turned to Patrick. "She is not living here. She just needed a safe place to stay."

"Right, I heard about those guys following her. Is she in some kind of trouble? Because Mom would understand that a whole lot easier than if you were just shacking up with her."

"Shut up, Patrick, it doesn't matter, because either way she is staying here, with me." He gave Macy a hard stare as if challenging her to say something different.

The microwave beeped, reminding him he was making dinner. Just great, Bryant thought, my brother shows up unannounced and now Macy's fully clothed, while I'm left standing in my underwear in the middle of the kitchen. He wondered if his night could get any worse, but then he imagined his mother showing up at his door. He knew things could always get worse.

"Can I stay and eat? I'm starving."

Knowing he wasn't going to get rid of his brother, he said, "If Macy doesn't mind, at this point, it's whatever. I'm going upstairs to change."

"Oh, good, I really didn't want to eat with you when you're in your underwear," Patrick yelled after Bryant.

122

"Go home if you don't like it," Brant yelled back.

Once Bryant left the room, Macy could feel Patrick looking at her. Macy's face turned red, and she went back to doing the dishes, to keep her busy. This time as she cleaned them she set out the plates and utensils they would need to eat. When she turned to set the table, she saw that Bryant's brother was still staring at her, and as much as she wanted to ignore it, she couldn't. "Why are you looking at me like that?"

"You're nice to look at, and I'm trying to figure out how you're going to make it in this family."

"What makes you so sure I'll be a part of your family, or that I even want to be?"

"Well, Macy, I'm going to let you in on a little secret. My brother doesn't bring girls home, ever. The fact that you're even here tells me a lot about how he feels about you."

"Well, he doesn't bring any girls home that you know about, anyway. He could have women here without your knowledge."

Patrick shook his head. "I don't think so, Macy. You're the first. And knowing that Bryant is willing to make a stand against Mom or Uncle Joe for you, well that tells me just how serious he is about you."

"Shut up, Patrick. I'm warning you for the last time," Bryant said. He stood in the open doorway, and who knew how long he'd been listening.

As they ate, Bryant kept the conversation on Patrick's favorite subject—himself. He wondered where Patrick's other half was, his twin brother, Gabriel. He hoped like hell that Gabe wasn't going to show up too, but usually where one of them went the other wasn't far behind. Sure enough, before Bryant knew it, his front door opened again.

"Bryant it's just me. I smell food," Bryant heard. The exact thing Bryant hadn't wanted to happen—Gabe came walking into the room. "Got room for one more?" he asked as he sat down. Immediately he started grabbing food off Patrick's plate.

"Hey, man, get your own plate," Patrick said, pulling his plate out of his brother's reach.

Gabe started to stand up, and that's when he noticed Macy sitting next to Bryant. "Well hello there. You must be Macy," he leaned over the table to shake her hand.

Bryant smacked his hand to his forehead and buried his face. He wanted to keep going until he slapped himself silly. When he looked over at Macy, he saw she was wide-eyed, looking at Patrick, and then back to Gabe.

"Wow, there are two of you," Macy said in amazement.

"Yep, didn't Bry tell you we're twins?"

"Well, yes, he did, but I didn't realize you looked exactly the same."

"I gave him his good looks," Gabe said. He stabbed a piece of steak to put on his plate.

"Did Patrick text you to tell you Macy was here?" Bryant already knew the answer, but he asked anyway.

"Nope, it's just the twin thing. I know when something's happening." He turned to Macy and looked her over. "You're pretty. I like her, Bry."

"Um, thank you, Gabe," Macy said. She turned to Bryant. "I'm going to get my stuff out of your truck and then head upstairs. I have a few more hours of work to do."

When she left the table, Macy heard Gabe say, "She's getting her stuff to do what? To stay?" Then she was out the door where she couldn't hear what Bryant said. Good—she didn't want to eavesdrop on their conversation.

When Macy tried to get her bags out of the bed of Bryant's truck, she found it more difficult then she'd anticipated. Climbing up on the bumper, she bent over, trying to hook her finger onto the strap of her backpack.

"Well, now there's a sight." Macy stood straight up as soon as she heard his voice. "Here, Macy, let me help you." Bryant was right behind her, and her butt was almost at his eye level. Putting his hands around her waist, he easily lifted her off the bumper. "You can get your satchel out of my back seat." When she returned, he started to apologize for his brothers, saying, "I'm sorry my family showed up and ruined our plans for the evening."

"Bryant, stop. You should never have to apologize for your family. I understand." Macy walked back inside as she said, "I'm going to get some work done up in your room, but I'll sleep on the couch if you put out a blanket and a pillow for me." Macy saw the twins standing in the kitchen doorway watching them. Bryant noticed them too.

"Macy, don't be silly. You don't need to sleep on the couch. You can have my bed, and I'll sleep on the couch." He kissed the top of her head.

"Good night, it was very nice to meet you both," she said to his bothers. They waved at Macy as she went up the stairs.

"You are totally sleeping with her, Bryant, so don't even try to bullshit us."

"You two are assholes you know that? Now get back in the kitchen. I'm going to kill both of you, and I want the blood in a place where I can easily clean it up."

They said in unison, "Oh shit."

Bryant sat back down at the table and shook his head at them. "Now tell me why you showed up at my door unannounced tonight, Patrick."

"Fred told me what was going on with the men at your 'friend's' apartment and with you asking him to call his friends at the police department. I knew you'd bring her here, so I came because I wanted to see her."

Bryant took a deep breath to calm himself. *His damn family.*

"Alright, your turn," he said, turning to Gabriel. "Why are you here?"

"Because Patrick texted me and I wanted to see her too."

"But you missed the best part!" Patrick exclaimed. "When I got here she was standing at the sink, washing dishes in just..." Bryant pointed his finger at Patrick, and that shut him up.

"You know he's just going to tell me later, right?" Gabe said.

"He won't tell you anything if he knows what's good for him, because if I hear one word about what he saw here tonight, then I'll know who to come after." Bryant knew he wasn't going to be able to hide Macy very much longer. Too many of his family members knew about her already. It wouldn't be long before his little sister, and his mother knew too.

Now if he could get rid of the twins so he could get back to her. She was finally upstairs in his bed, right now, and he was sitting around with his brothers. There were times when having a close-knit family was great, but tonight Bryant wished he lived in Siberia, far away from the lot of them, because he didn't want or need them in his business.

Macy didn't know how long Bryant would take, so she got ready for bed and climbed under his covers. She spread her notes out across the bed and opened her laptop. Surprisingly enough, she felt very comfortable there. Looking around his room again, she could imagine pretty curtains on the windows, and two wingback chairs by the fireplace with a nice soft rug in between. She could picture making love with Bryant in front of a raging fire, then snuggling under a cozy blanket.

Macy knew she was getting too far ahead of herself. She wanted to help him fix the house up, but she had no idea what that would take. She'd never even held a hammer or a drill, but somehow, she knew that with Bryant it would be fun. Closing her eyes, Macy imagined Bryant standing behind her, helping her hold a drill while she drove a screw into the wall to hang a picture—their wedding portrait.

She opened her eyes and shook her head. What was she thinking? It was one thing to fantasize about helping Bryant renovate the house, but it was a whole other thing to daydream about marriage. Then, what about that image of children playing in the backyard she'd seen earlier, well, maybe they weren't her kids she'd pictured. Maybe she could see that the house could use some kids running around in it. She told herself these things, so she didn't have to face the feelings she was beginning to have for Bryant.

{12}

Macy looked back down at her computer screen. She tried to distract herself by getting back into her story. That's what she needed, to comb over her notes. Macy knew she was missing something, but she wasn't sure what.

When she'd asked Mr. Smith at the club on Friday about the club's surveillance footage, he had told her that the police had looked at the video and didn't find anything. Why didn't they see the girls leave the club? She was going to have to get her hands on those tapes, to see for herself. It was possible that the club had doctored the videotape. Macy wasn't a technician or anything, but even she could spot the little blip that happened when a tape-recording stopped and started again. It was possible that the police had looked for that sort of thing too, but she had to assuage her curiosity.

On the other hand, what if the police had only looked at the video for the night the girls went missing? The girls could have been moved to another location later, maybe within containers to conceal their identity. Macy had so many questions and no answers, was it possible that the girls had never left the club at all? But with those two guys chasing her, she felt she had to be getting close. She knew she needed to get her hands on the tapes, and she still needed to do a little of her own surveillance. The last two nights she had planned to do just that, but something, or someone, got in the way.

She needed to get her mind back on her job, and off the sexy construction worker. Once she solved the mystery of the missing girls, she could give her undivided attention to Bryant and see just where this was going with him—when he wasn't protecting her, or saving her from those two big goons.

Was that what attracted him to her? Was it the damsel in distress situations she kept getting into? Or did he feel the need to take care of her because she always needed his help? That certainly would make more sense than Bryant actually being attracted to her. Macy was plain—there was no doubt about it. She liked to think she was simply easy-going, that she just was who she was, and most guys didn't find that attractive.

Bryant was not only gorgeous, but he was the most down-to-earth guy she had ever met, and he clearly loved his family. Not too many guys would let their brothers stand in the way of a sure thing, especially when the woman was already waiting for him in his bed. Unless he was afraid to come to bed with her and was using the twins as an excuse.

Either way, Macy had to get up early the next day and needed to get some sleep. If Bryant wanted to wake her, then he would. Closing her computer and collecting her notes, Macy put everything on his nightstand. She was tempted to look inside the nightstand's drawer to see if he kept condoms there, but instead, she turned out the light so she wouldn't look.

Bryant finally got his twin brothers to go back to their dorm room for the night. As soon as they left, he locked the door behind them and ran for the stairs. When he opened the bedroom door the room was dark inside—shit, she was already asleep.

He slipped into the room, thinking maybe he should grab a pillow and sleep on the couch. As he stripped down to his boxers, he debated whether he should disturb Macy. He walked to the side of the bed where she was sleeping. In the dim light from the window, he could see that she had one hand tucked under her chin while the other poked out from the side of her pillow.

Bryant knew it was creepy to stand over Macy watching her sleep, but he liked seeing her look so peaceful. As his eyes adjusted to the darkness, he could see more of her. She had one foot sticking out from under the covers at the edge of the bed. His fingers ached to touch her smooth skin, but he didn't dare disturb her. Just then, she stirred and rolled over, and Bryant stood back and held his breath—had he woken her? Then she settled into her sleep again. He walked to the other side of the bed and slipped in between the covers. She said his name.

"Yeah, it's me," he whispered. "Do you want me to sleep on the couch?" When he heard a sleepy "no" he sighed with relief, and once he was fully under the covers, she nestled into him. He couldn't help the feeling that came over him, being in his bed with Macy snuggled up next to him. Macy was right where she belonged. He knew tonight wouldn't be the night they made love, but somehow, holding her like this was just as good. The things that comforted him were listening to her breathe and smelling her hair. Bryant closed his eyes. He couldn't think of any other place he would rather be.

The next morning, they woke early to the sound of his doorbell ringing. Bryant jumped up to put on pants to answer the door. Whoever was out there wasn't going to go away. He looked out the window and saw his father's car in the driveway. Shit. Bryant knew what was coming next.

When he got downstairs, Bryant took a blanket off the back of the couch and tried to make it look as if he'd slept there last night. Then he opened the door onto his parents, who both stood on his front porch.

"Mom, Dad? What are you doing here so early? Is everything alright?" Bryant knew exactly why they had come, but he wasn't going to let on.

"May we come in, Bryant?" his mother asked.

Stepping back, he said, "Of course, come in." He watched as his mother noticed the crumpled blanket on the couch.

"Is there something wrong with your bed?" Arlene asked, gesturing toward the blanket.

"Mother, I'm sure you know what's wrong with my bed. Otherwise, you wouldn't be here. Good morning, Dad." His father stood by the door and waited.

His mother sighed, "Well, I guess I do know. So, you have a guest staying here with you. Is that how you walk around when you have female company at your house?" Bryant was standing in only jeans, with no shirt.

"I was sleeping. I threw some pants on to answer the door." It was Bryant's house to walk around as he chose, but he couldn't say that to his mother. His father chuckled from behind him. Were they going to ask him whether he'd slept with Macy? He didn't plan to volunteer any information. Besides, he'd only slept next to her. It wasn't as if he had sex with her.

"When were you going to tell us that you had someone staying with you? And when did you plan on introducing her to us?"

Just then, there were footsteps, and Bryant heard Macy on the stairs. He hoped she had clothes on. "I guess right now," Bryant said as Macy walked into the room.

"Mom, Dad, this is Macy Greene. Macy, this is my Mom, Arlene, and my Father, Cadman." Macy stepped up to shake his mother's hand.

"Nice to meet you, Mrs. O'Shea, Bryant has told me so much about you and your family. I think it's fascinating that he has such a big family. I'm an only child." Cadman stepped away from the door. As Macy went to shake his hand, he hugged her.

"Nice to finally meet you, Macy, we've heard a lot about you, too." That made Macy blush, and Cadman quickly said, "Good things, of course."

Arlene interrupted her husband, "Macy, will you be joining us for Sunday Mass and dinner this weekend?"

Bryant had known the invitation was coming, but when Macy said she would love to come, it floored him. It took him a second to recover, and then he noticed that his mother was smiling. Yeah, she'd gotten what she wanted.

"Well, Cadman, we'd better let them get ready for work," his mother said. "I will see you on Sunday," she said, kissing Bryant. Turning to Macy, she said, "It was lovely to meet you." She walked out the door while Cadman said goodbye to Macy and hugged her again. When he walked to his son, Cadman quietly said, "You know you're not fooling anybody with that blanket. Your mother is smarter than that."

Yeah, Bryant knew his mother was aware he'd spent the night with Macy. But she hadn't directly asked him about it, so Bryant didn't need to lie. He couldn't believe he was a grown man, and yet he still had to answer to his mother.

After they left, Macy said, "The blanket on the couch is a nice touch. Do you think they fell for it?"

"Not one bit. But if my mother wanted to know, she would have asked." He took Macy in his arms and smiled down at her. "Good morning," he said, kissing her. He could taste that she'd brushed her teeth and was all minty, but she hadn't put on any makeup yet. He liked her this way. "Sorry, last night didn't go as planned. But, I did like having you snuggled up against me."

"Snuggled against you, huh? Is that your way of saying I hogged the bed? Because at my place, the bed is all mine," she said playfully.

"I'm glad that you don't share your bed at home. I wasn't insinuating anything. I loved having you in my bed last night. I want to have you, in my bed, more," he said as he started walking her backward in the direction of the stairs.

"I can't. I have to be at work in an hour." She kissed him teasingly.

"We have some time. I'm sure I could make you feel good before work." He bent and put his shoulder in her middle. Standing, he lifted her over his shoulder, so she was draped over his back. He loved it when she squealed. He was going to like having her live with him, no matter what his mother, his uncle, or anyone else thought.

He took her upstairs and placed her in the middle of the bed. "Now I am going to watch you lose your mind." He climbed up her body, kissing his way up. He knew they didn't have the time he wanted to dedicate to properly loving her body, but he could still work a little magic before they started their days.

Slowly he opened her blouse, kissing the skin he uncovered until the shirt was open to her waist. Sliding the cup of her bra down to expose her breast to him, he touched his lips to her skin just as his phone went off. He put his forehead to her chest and took a deep breath. He'd let it go to voicemail. He tried to ignore the noise it was making and continue with Macy, but the phone rang again. Macy laughed.

"How much do you want to bet that that's your Uncle Joe calling?" she asked, re-buttoning her shirt and squirming away from him.

"You know Macy, you are so lucky you're an only child. I kind of wish I was right now. The twins, my parents, now the phone, tonight after we get back from investigating, I'm turning off my phone and locking the doors and windows so we won't be disturbed."

Macy stood and walked out of the room, saying, "Promises, promises."

Bryant smacked the empty bed next to him and let out a frustrated sigh. A cold shower it is, he thought.

Bryant dropped Macy off in front of her office building. He was in a bad mood. Today was going to be a very long day, with a lot of work to be done before he could come back to pick Macy up. She wasn't sure when she'd finish work, and he didn't want her to leave the building without him.

She had resisted his restrictions, but once he explained that those men who were out to get her probably knew where she worked and could follow her once she left the safety of her building, then she came around. She'd wanted to go to the police station to get the surveillance video she'd been after, but with Bryant's insistence that she not leave, Macy said she'd have to call her cop friend and see if he could send it to her instead.

Macy still wanted to know if there were tapes from the other five clubs, and if there were, then she'd need to watch them, too. Bryant was going to try to help her by calling in some favors. But really, Bryant had enough of his own work to do.

The phone call that morning had been from his foreman, who wasn't going to be coming to the job site that day. His daughter was sick at home, and last time he'd had a sick kid, his wife had taken the day off. Now it was Mark's turn.

All Bryant wanted was for his day to be over, and to be home again with Macy. He wasn't kidding when he'd said he was locking the doors. There was no way he was going to let a family member waltz in and interrupt them again. With his luck, it would be his sisters this time.

As usual, Macy was the first one at her desk that morning. She planned to use her time alone in the office to make her phone call to the police without anyone overhearing. She dialed the number of her police contact and secret informant, also known as Bobby, and waited for him to answer.

"Detective Bobby Hernandez," said the voice on the other end of the phone.

"Bobby, it's me, Macy Greene. I need a favor." Macy stood in her cubicle, where she could make sure that no one who walked into the office could hear her.

"Macy Greene," Bobby said, "what can I do for you today? Or rather, what can I do that won't get me fired? It seems every time I hear from you. You need something that could get me into trouble with my superiors."

Bobby and Macy had gone to school together, and he'd had a crush on her a long time ago. She didn't like exploiting her connection to get information, but she was desperate to see the surveillance footage.

"I know you guys have video surveillance of the doors at the nightclub, and some footage from the cameras inside." She didn't know if they had any tape from the inside of the club, but she figured it couldn't hurt to try. "I need to look at those tapes." She held her breath and waited for him to reply.

"And how am I supposed to do that, Macy?"

"Can you email me the files?" Again, he didn't say anything, so she added, "Please?"

"When I lose my job for leaking information to the press, I'm going to come live with you and mooch off of you," he said. Macy didn't know what to say, especially because he was attracted to her. Bobby sensed the awkward moment. "I'm just kidding, Macy. Give me some time, and I'll send them over to you."

Macy let out a breath she hadn't realized she'd been holding.

"Bobby, you're the best, but I need one more thing, one teeny, tiny thing." She heard him laugh on the other end.

"Now why do I have the feeling that this one is really going to get me into trouble? Okay, hit me. I'll see what I can do, but I'm not making any promises."

"I need to get my hands on the surveillance footage from the other nightclubs too, all five of the others, if you can manage that."

"Macy, Macy, Macy," he sighed. "This is going to cost you big time. This favor is definitely worth the dinner I keep asking you to have with me."

Bryant wasn't going to like that, so Macy asked, "How about drinks instead? I'll buy."

Laughing, Bobby said, "Really, you're trying to negotiate after asking for favors?"

"Well of course. You didn't expect me to take the first thing you offer, did you?"

"Alright then, I reject your offer for drinks. My counteroffer is lunch. I pay."

"Deal, just as long as you know we're only meeting as friends." Macy didn't want to lead him on knowing that Bobby liked her, and especially with Bryant in the picture.

"One day, Macy, you will go out with me, and not just as friends. But don't worry, I'm a patient man."

"Bobby," she said with mock annoyance.

"I know, Macy, I know. But a man can dream, can't he?"

She ended the call and started up her computer so she would be ready the moment Bobby sent the video files. The only problem was finding some privacy to watch the videos. Being stuck in the office, she couldn't watch them at her desk. She worried she might have to wait until she got home—or rather, back to Bryant's house—where she could study them in peace.

He sat at his desk, listening to his goons making excuses. He needed them for their muscle, but the men were clearly morons. Twice now, that woman, Macy Greene, had managed to give them the slip. How hard could it be to catch one stupid bitch and bring her to him? He should never have allowed her to leave his office in the first place, but then again, he hadn't thought her investigation would get very far. No one had looked that closely to missing people in a city of this size because there were bigger crimes to investigate. Until now that is, and that was why he needed Ms. Greene in his office right away before she could tell anyone and bring his empire down. *No, I can't have that, now can I?*

Mr. Smith knew that the reporter had been looking into public records at the tax clerk's office, and she must know by now about the different corporations that owned his clubs, at least on paper.

It was a good thing that he kept someone at the tax office on his payroll. Without that inside man, he wouldn't have known that Macy Greene had gone snooping around about his companies. To do her prying, she'd had to show her ID. Now, thanks to his man at the tax office, Mr. Smith had a copy of Macy Greene's driver's license sitting right there on the desk in front of him.

That first night, when she'd come to the club asking questions, he'd just wanted to know who she was and what she really wanted. He'd had his guys follow her out of the club, but she'd ditched them somehow in a bar bathroom. She must have known they were there, this woman was smarter then she looked.

Once Mr. Smith knew she was digging deeper into things that weren't any of her business, he wanted her brought to him. He wanted to make her sorry for sticking her pretty little nose where it didn't belong. She was the strong, stern librarian type—he'll love to break down that strong-willed front she put on and make her beg. Maybe he'd even keep her for himself, at least until he got tired of her. He could picture her before him on her knees, pleasing him, looking up at him through those thick-rimmed glasses as he squeezed her jaw, forcing her to bring him ultimate pleasure. He would watch as he saw panic in her eyes when he pushed deeper into her mouth, not allowing her to breathe. *Yes, oh how I'm going to enjoy that.*

"Find her," he told his thugs. "I want her in my office, or you're not going to like your life when I'm done with you. Do you understand what I'm saying?" Both men grumbled and nodded as they left the office.

Mr. Smith went behind his desk and walked to a concealed door. He pushed a button, and a secret door slid open. He disappeared into what was, for many, the depths of hell. Determined to get his satisfaction, even if he had to go through every girl he had, Mr. Smith entered his discipline room and thoughtfully examined the items there, wondering what would please him most that day.

{13}

Bryant had a grueling day at work without his foreman on site, but the thought of picking Macy up from work and then going home together got him through his day. He couldn't wait to hold her in his arms and to get her naked again. Nothing would get in their way this time.

Driving to pick her up from her office, he thought about what he should get for dinner. He realized he didn't turely know what she liked. The night he brought dinner to her apartment, he'd brought a variety of fast food, and she'd eaten the burger. They'd had pizza together, and steak. Burgers weren't very romantic, but they were a safe bet. It didn't matter what they ate, so long as they had enough food to fuel their passions for later, and he hoped it wasn't too much later.

At the drive-thru window, Bryant ordered the same thing he had the last time. With the food already in hand, he went to pick Macy up. He parked and went to get his girl. His girl—he liked the sound of that. He shook off the dust and dirt from his clothes all the way down to his work boots and then went into the building to find her.

Standing in the doorway, Bryant looked the room over. He saw only men moving about. No one seemed to pay much attention to him, so he started walking down the aisle of cubicles, hoping to see her sitting at her desk. He found her staring at her computer with her brow creased as if she was deep in thought. Macy was so focused on her work, she didn't see Bryant standing there. The guy behind her saw him, though, and asked, "Can I help you?" Macy jumped a little and looked up to see Bryant.

"What are you doing here?" she asked.

"It's time to go home," he said. Macy turned to look at the man in the cubicle behind her, who stood there as if he didn't care that he was obviously listening to their conversation.

"I didn't realize it had gotten so late. Let me just shut down my computer, and I'll be right with you."

Bryant introduced himself to the man, putting out his hand and saying, "Hi, I'm Bryant, Macy's boyfriend." When the two men shook, Jimmy's hand was dwarfed Bryant's larger, stronger hand.

"I'm Jimmy," the other man said. When Bryant heard the name, he started to squeeze the man's hand. This man was the dick that had been on Macy's recording, talking about her, asking her to dinner.

When Jimmy pulled his hand away, he rubbed it as if it was sore from Bryant's handshake. *You'd better keep your comments to yourself next time,* Bryant thought, *or I might do a lot worse like maybe knock out some teeth.* Macy stood looking from one man to the other.

"I'm ready to go now," she said.

Bryant turned to Jimmy, "Nice to meet you." He put his arm around Macy as they left the office.

"What was that about?" Macy asked when they got outside. "For a minute I thought you were going to pee on my leg or something, to mark me as yours."

Bryant laughed. "Yeah, something like that. I just wanted him to know that if he has another slip of the lip, I'll be back."

"Oh, I forgot you heard him on the recording. You know I can handle him, right?"

"I'm sure you can. You're a strong woman, but you shouldn't have to handle him. He should act like a gentleman and not be disrespectful towards a woman in the first place."

Macy smiled at him and said, "I remember when you tried to pass yourself off as a gentleman." Bryant tried not to smile as he remembered that first night in her apartment.

The ride to his house felt like it took forever. The traffic out of the city was horrible, even once they hit the highway. It didn't help he'd been looking forward to getting her home and having her all to himself.

They ate dinner as he drove, and told each other the events of their day. Macy told Bryant all about Bobby and how he was the one who could get the videos from The Black Dragon, the nightclub where so many underage kids went, and which Mr. Smith supposedly owned. She explained that the other nightclubs weren't in Bobby's jurisdiction, but that he was trying to get the footage for her anyway, which was a huge favor.

Bryant wondered how well she knew this Bobby guy, and how good of a friend he truly was. Would she owe him for this favor? He felt tightness in his chest as jealousy crept in. As Macy kept on talking about the nightclubs and her story, he was dying to ask if there was ever anything more than friendship between them. He knew it wasn't any of his business, but that didn't necessarily help stop his curiosity.

"If he could get those tapes it would answer a lot of questions," she was saying. "I mean, what if on all the tapes you never see any of the girls leave? Then either the girls are still there, or they held them until they could move them at another time. I was thinking about this last night in bed while I was waiting for you. If the police only looked at the tapes from the night the girls disappeared, then they might not have seen the girls leave. But I don't think they'd keep the girls in the club, necessarily. What if the police came back to do another search? This favor will be worth drinks and lunch if Bobby can deliver."

"What do you mean, drinks and lunch?" Bryant glanced over at her. Macy winced and looked out the window.

"I made a deal with him, but Bobby and I are only friends. I made that very clear to him that this is not a date."

"Um, okay, well it sounds like a date to me. Drinks where?" That jealous knot in his chest felt ready to explode.

"Hey, don't sound so righteous. If I recall correctly, you owed that Angela woman a favor for helping me at the pub. The way your sister made it sound like Angela might want more than drinks and lunch from you. That's nothing like having drinks as a friend with a professional contact. I never asked how you thanked Angela, even if I did think about it because I had no right to ask. I'm telling you there is nothing between Bobby and me. I'm not that kind of person, and if you think I'd do something like that—"

They had come to a stoplight on the roadway. Bryant leaned over and interrupted her with a quick kiss on the lips to stop her rant. So, she had been jealous of him, too. Interesting.

"I don't think anything is going on between you two, but I want to make sure that he knows that, and you do have the right to know what I did to thank Angela. I had my crew build an entertainment center for her living room. I sent two of my guys over to her place, and they had it all done in a day."

Macy took his hand as they started driving again. "I'm sorry. I didn't mean to go off like that. It's just... I don't like it when someone questions my integrity, and I assure you, I made myself perfectly clear on the phone with Bobby that we would go out as friends only. When we were in school, a long, long time ago, he had a crush on me, but I don't use that in my favor. I would never lead him on to get him to do something for me."

"Okay, I get that you might have made it clear to him, but I have to wonder—who suggested drinks and lunch? You or him?"

"I did, because he originally asked for dinner, and that was too much the like a date."

"See, he's still crushing on you. I'm sure that's why he helps you out. Because he's hoping that one of these times he'll be able to convince you to go out with him. Don't get me wrong, because I do understand his reasoning. I pushed my way into your life too, because the moment you kissed me, I knew, I had to kiss you again and again."

"If I remember correctly, I pulled you into my life—you didn't push your way into mine. I asked for your help, and then I kissed you."

He squeezed her hand, liking the sound of that. They weren't far from his house, and he hoped they could pick up where they'd left off earlier that morning. First, he would need to lock up the house and turn off his phone.

The driveway was empty, which was a relief. Bryant parked the truck, pulling Macy close to his side before she could get out. Taking her chin in his fingers, he kissed her—a long, soft, tender kiss. When he pulled back, he apologized. "I'm sorry, Macy. I wasn't questioning your integrity as much as I was his. I want you to be mine, and I know how men think." Macy laughed.

"I'm serious," Bryant said, "I don't want anyone to come on to you, or behave disrespectfully towards you in any way. In your office, I wanted that guy to know that you have me now. I heard some of the things that asshole said about you, and I wanted to kick his ass. It's my job to protect you."

Macy thought, *there it is, so he does think I'm a damsel in distress. Even if that's sweet,* she couldn't allow him to think she needed rescuing. He wasn't her prince, riding in to save her from the bad men in his white pickup truck.

"Bryant, you know I don't need to be rescued. I may be a woman, but I'm not completely helpless."

"You are definitely a woman. A very beautiful woman. A woman most men would like to be with, and I can't have them stealing you away from me, now can I?"

He was making light of her words. Meanwhile, Macy was still concerned about why he wanted to be with her.

"Let's go inside, so I can show you how I treat a beautiful woman." He took her hand and slid her across the truck's bench seat, pulling her right out of the door with him.

Macy couldn't deny that she wanted to be with Bryant, and not just physically, but she needed to level the playing field. If he thought she always needed saving, eventually he would think she was helpless. Macy hated to seem weak. She needed to prove to him that she could take care of herself. She felt they were compatible, and could even see things working out for them in the future, but first Bryant would have to get over his Prince Charming complex.

Once they made it inside the house, Bryant kicked off his smelly work boots, locked the door, and checked the windows. Taking her hand, he led her up the stairs and into his bathroom, where they stood looking at one another.

Bryant pulled his phone from his pocket and made a show of turning it off. He wasn't going to let anyone interrupt them this time. He wanted to touch her, but he was dirty and dusty from working all day, so he started to remove his clothes while she stood and watched. The heat of her gaze made him feel extremely turned on. Slowly, he teased her, letting each article of clothing drop to the floor one by one, until he stood in front of her completely naked.

When she moved to touch him, Bryant stopped her. He took her hand and guided it to the hem of her shirt, wordlessly letting her know what he wanted. When she understood his meaning and began to remove her clothes, Bryant watched just as intently as she'd done with him. Watching her as she slowly stripped, teasing him with each article of clothing as he had done for her, made him even harder than he already was.

Her shirt hit the floor, and then her bra. Bryant's eyes latched onto her hard nipples, and his hands itched to touch her, but he was still filthy from work. Now her slacks were sliding to the floor, and then, finally, her panties.

"Let's get into the shower," he said, "I'm dirty from work."

"I can fix that for you," Macy grinned. He knew just how good that would be.

"Yes, I'm well aware," he teased, "but remember—when it's my turn, I will show no mercy."

"Promises, promises," she said, stepping into the shower. Bryant smacked her bottom and then smiled when she let out a surprised squeal. So far, there wasn't a single thing about Macy Green he didn't like. She was sexy, strong, smart, and independent. Climbing in behind her, he began adjusting the water.

Once the water was nice and hot, Bryant stood beneath it to get wet and handed Macy the soap. He knew now that he'd given her free rein, she was going to take full advantage. She lathered the soap in her hands, then, starting with his chest, she ran her hands over his shoulders, then worked her way down. When she reached his nipples, she allowed her nails to scrape gently over them, sending a jolt straight through him.

Bryant closed his eyes and held his breath as Macy's hands spread the lather over his abs and then up his sides. Her slow pursuit of his body was killing him, but it was thrilling just the same. Gliding her hands down his arm, then back up, she guided his hands to the back of his head before running her hands over his armpits. Her fingers sliding through his hair felt so surreal and intimate. He heard her whisper that he should keep his hands right where they were, on his head. She was driving him crazy. He could almost come just from her touching him—he was that close.

Macy moved her hands to his back, working, every hard muscle she found as her fingers massaged his skin. The moan he made told her that he liked what she was doing to him. If he'd only known what Macy had in store for him, he never would have been able to stand still.

Macy massaged her fingers over his butt, handsome and firm like the rest of him. As she rubbed, she dipped her head down until she was looking straight at the largest penis she'd ever seen. Taking a deep breath, she licked the tip.

Bryant's eyes flew open, and he looked down at Macy, who locked eyes with him as she took him into her mouth. He closed his eyes again and leaned his head back, as he said her name. It felt like he was dreaming.

She tried to take as much of him into her mouth as she could, but she didn't come close to taking all of him. With her hand, she held him at the base as she worked the rest. It didn't take long before he pulled her up from her perch in front of him and kissed her hard—a greedy kiss that took her whole mouth, tongue, and lips.

With his rough hands, he showed her how wild he was for her. She loved it. His touch on her soft skin made her want to jump him right there in the shower. It surprised her to hear the water turn off. He took her hand and pulled her from the shower without even bothering to grab towels. Still wet, he picked Macy up and wrapped her legs around his waist. After walking them to his bed, he placed her in the middle.

"I have to taste you," he said, "and then I'm going to make love to you, Macy. I can't wait any longer." He scrambled onto the bed and slid between her legs. As he gently spread her legs, Macy held her breath and watched him. He slowly moved his face to her hips and kissed his way around her skin, nibbling, as his mouth got closer to where she wanted him. She felt his fingers move through her wetness as he opened her to him, and when his tongue finally touched her, she almost jumped off the bed. Grabbing the covers with both hands, Macy arched her back as every muscle in her body tightened. Even her butt lifted off the bed, and at that moment, Bryant slid his hands under her bottom and pulled her into him. His tongue flicked over her for a moment, and then he stopped and sucked. The sensation of him switching back sent her over the edge.

As her body throbbed, Bryant stayed with her, slowing his pace but not stopping until she had to pull him free. He kissed his way up her body, stopping at her breasts.

"Do you have any idea what you do to me? I want to be inside of you so badly, and yet, I know I should wait."

"Wait, no. What? No, you shouldn't wait."

"Macy, would it scare you off if I told you how much I like you?"

"Bryant, stop talking. You locked the doors. You turned off your phone. Come on, please, I need you now."

When Bryant heard the urgency in Macy's voice, he knew he couldn't deny her. Reaching into his nightstand, he pulled out a full box of condoms. As he opened it, he watched her face. He wanted her to know this wasn't his norm.

"I should say one more thing before we do this. I want you to know that I don't make this a habit—bringing women to my home." When Macy's brow furrowed, he thought he might have said something wrong. "What I'm saying is you're the first, ever, to be in my bed."

Macy remembered what his brother Patrick had said about Bryant never having women in his house. She hadn't believed him at the time, but now, looking at Bryant, she knew it was the truth. She pulled him down to her. "Thank you for telling me. Now kiss me."

Their kiss grew deeper, as Macy rolled him onto his back, she took over. He made her feel like the aggressor, which was something she'd never experienced before. The newfound power fed her need to have Bryant inside of her. Breaking the kiss, she reached for the box of condoms and pulled one free.

"Macy, wait," he said, putting his hand over hers to stop her from opening the wrapper.

Closing her eyes, she sighed. They'd been close, so damn close. She didn't open her eyes as she waited for Bryant to make the next move. Maybe he'd changed his mind. At this point, she didn't think it was ever actually going to happen between them. Taking in a deep breath in an attempt to tamp down the anger that was growing inside her, Macy waited. Bryant said nothing.

She couldn't take it anymore, so she got off the bed. Needing space, she went into the bathroom, gathered her clothes from the floor, and started to get dressed. She wasn't surprised when she heard Bryant knock on the door.

"Macy, listen, I'm sorry. I didn't mean to do that. I just don't want to rush things."

She laughed because usually putting the brakes on sex was something she did, not something the man did. He made her feel as if she was pushing him into something he didn't want. If she stayed with him like this much longer, she was going to go crazy. It might be time to go home.

Once she was fully clothed, Macy opened the door. She walked past his naked body, trying not to look at him, and started to collect her belongings. Stuffing everything back into her bags, she looked around the room again to see if she'd forgotten anything. She avoided looking at him, though.

He followed her and asked, "Macy, what are you doing?"

"I think it might be time for me to leave," she said. "I have to get back to working on the missing girls."

"Macy, listen, it's not safe for you to go home right now."

"Look, Bryant, I think you have this idea in your head that it's your job to protect me. Well, it isn't, because I can take care of myself." For a second time, he put his hand over hers, this time to stop her from leaving.

"I don't want you to go." He pulled her bag out of her hands and dropped it to the floor. Sliding his arms around her and holding her close, he said, "I don't think you understand why I stopped you."

"I have a few ideas, and I really don't want to hear you say them aloud." She tried to pull free, hoping to avoid this particular embarrassment. She didn't need to hear his reasons why he didn't want to be with her.

The hurt in Macy's eyes hit Bryant hard, "I can see that I hurt your feelings. That's the last thing I ever wanted to do. But I still needed to stop you, so that I could tell you something before we went any further."

"I think we should chalk it up to the fact that we just don't fit well together. My feelings aren't hurt," Macy released a loud breath. "I'm just frustrated. I'll call a cab and go to a friend's place, so you don't have to worry about me. Thank you for all your help, but I can take it from here."

"Macy, I can't let you leave."

That got her attention. "What do you mean? You can't, or you won't? You can't keep me here against my will."

He didn't want her to leave without hearing him out. "Please, sit with me. I don't plan on keeping you here if you truly don't want to be here, but at least hear me out first."

"At least put on some clothes, then, please." Macy put her hand to her forehead and let out a loud breath.

{14}

Bryant went to his dresser and pulled out a clean pair of boxers. He slipped them on and went over to the bed where she sat. "Macy, you know that I'm Catholic, and I take my religion very seriously. I'm not perfect by any means, but I never want what we share to be just physical. The last few days, the time I've spent with you has been great, and I don't want to be with anyone else." He sighed and took her hand. "What I'm trying to say is that I'm falling for you, Macy. That's what makes you different from anyone else. So, you see, my physical need to be with you, is messing with my moral strength."

"Have you been talking to your uncle again? I swear you make me feel like the devil, I'm pulling you into the dark side. Bryant, look, I don't want you to do anything that would go against your beliefs, but you send all kinds of mixed signals. I can't wrap my head around it sometimes. I'm never the one who initiates sex, but the way you make me feel... You drive me crazy, and you leave me needy, frustrated. I'm not particularly fond of feeling that way. Sometimes it's as if I'm the man pushing myself on you, and I don't like that either."

"I realize my behavior doesn't make any sense to you, and sometimes I don't understand it either. I want you, but the thing is that I want all of you—heart, body, and soul."

"Bryant, the things you're asking for don't happen overnight, or in our case, a few days."

"I know I've been trying to take things out of order. I should at least have your heart before I ask for anything else. Although, knowing that doesn't make me want you any less."

"I knew that living under the same roof with you was going to be too hard. Bryant, I think I should leave and give you your space."

"Macy, I don't want you to leave. I told you—" but he was interrupted by Macy's phone going off.

Macy went downstairs to retrieve her phone from her bag, leaving Bryant sitting on the bed, wondering what was wrong with him. All he'd been able to think about for days was getting Macy naked, but every time they came close to sealing the deal, he'd put a stop to it.

He understood how Macy felt about him sending mixed signals because he was annoyed with himself for the same reason. He wanted her very badly, there was no doubt, but when it came to the intimacy, he was a little scared—she would think he was crazy if she knew how he saw their future together. He had strong feelings for her, but he didn't want to scare her off.

Bryant snapped out of his trance when he heard Macy yelling. Rushing down the stairs, he wondered what could be wrong. He found her pacing in the living room, making agitated movements. He tried to listen to her side of the conversation.

"No, please don't go into the hallway. Mrs. Wilkins—yes, I understand, but you've called the police, now you need to let them handle it, okay? Yes, ma'am… No, but, I don't want you to get hurt. I'll be there just as soon as I can. Thank you for calling me."

Macy hung up the phone and collapsed onto the couch, sinking her head between her knees. She didn't know how to deal with the anger that surged through her body just then. Bryant came to her side and started rubbing her back. It helped some, but taking deep breaths helped more.

Bryant didn't even really need to ask. "What's happened, Macy? Did they break into your apartment?"

Her head popped up so quickly she almost head-butted Bryant. "That was Mrs. Wilkins. She said it looks like they kicked in my door. Not that they're going to find what they're looking for, but still, it leaves my apartment wide open for anyone to take anything they want."

Bryant said very calmly, "Call your friend Bobby and have him meet me at your place. I'll fix your door, but I want you to stay here, where it's safe." She started to protest, but he stopped her. "Hear me out. What if they didn't break in to find what you're working on, but so they could find where you're staying? This could be a trap. Once they see you going into your building, all they have to do is wait for you to leave and follow us here. Now, I'm a contractor, so I go around fixing doors all the time. I won't look suspicious to them. I want you to call your detective friend and fill him in on the situation. See what he thinks about everything that's been going on since you started looking into those missing girls."

She opened her mouth, and then shut it. Maybe she hadn't considered that they weren't after her notes or her computer—they could be after her. "Macy, one more thing, and I know you're not going to like it, but for my peace of mind, I'm going to call one of my brothers and ask him to stay with you until I get back. There's a chance they could have followed us here from your office or something, and they're just waiting for me to leave you here alone." Bryant waited for that to sink in and then added, "Now, I'm going to run and get dressed. You call your friend at the police station."

Macy watched Bryant take the stairs two at a time, his broad shoulders bunched and pulled as he gripped the handrail. She hadn't said a word since Bryant pointed out that the men could already know she was hiding out here, with him. Now, she'd put him in danger too. Macy didn't want anyone to get hurt. All she wanted was to find the missing girls, prove they hadn't been runaways, and break her big story as a serious journalist.

She started looking for Bobby's home number since he would have left work at that time. It wasn't more than ten minutes until Bryant was back, fully dressed, with his phone to his ear. Whoever he was speaking to, it was an intense conversation. He was practically yelling into the phone. Macy's eyes tracked his movements as he paced from one side of the room to the other, much as she'd done earlier when she'd been on the phone.

Grabbing his boots, he sat next to her and slipped them on, saying into the phone, "Yes it's important. I wouldn't be asking if it wasn't. Okay. See you then." He shoved the phone back into his pocket then turned to Macy. "My brother Paul is coming. You saw him on Friday night at the pub. He was the bouncer, and he'll keep you safe. I don't want you to worry about your apartment, okay. I'll make sure it's secure."

But by then she wasn't worried about the apartment as much as she was worried about Bryant. "You do realize that now I've put you in danger," she said.

"I don't think they know that you're here, not yet, anyway. But even if they did, Paul will be with you. Really, he is coming more for me than he is for you. With him here, I know that you're safe and sound."

"But when did keeping me safe become your job? I don't want you to think I can't take care of myself."

Bryant took her left hand and toyed with her ring finger. "Macy, I don't see you as weak. I see you as a strong woman, a force to be reckoned with, and a beautiful woman, too. But strong or not, I'm not going to stand back and let someone hurt you. We might have been thrown together by your investigation, but I like to think of it as fate. There's a reason you ran into my family's pub that night. Caring about you is important to me. You are important to me." He sighed and looked into her eyes. "I guess what I'm trying to say here is, I'm having trouble with the physical relationship because I want this to go right between us. I don't know if that makes any sense to you?"

As he spoke, Macy watched him playing with her ring finger. She realized the significance of his movements. Was he implying he wanted to marry her? He said he'd wanted more from her than just sex, but she knew that "more" only came with time, and their relationship was so new—they were still learning about each other.

A knock at Bryant's door halted the conversation and thoughts about marriage. Bryant kissed her and got up to answer the knock. In the doorway stood a man even bigger than Bryant. He had the same family resemblance she'd seen in the photos upstairs, so Macy knew it must be his brother Paul. Bryant welcomed him in with a quick embrace and then introduced him to Macy.

Macy stood to shake Paul's hand, and she realized how tall he was because she didn't even come up to his shoulders. When he hugged her, it lifted her right off her feet, taking her off guard. Macy gasped as all of the air in her lungs squeezed out of her. "Okay, Paul, that's enough," she heard Bryant say. "Put her down before you break her."

Macy felt a little dizzy—from the lack of air, she was sure. As cute and well-built as Paul was, he didn't make her heart go crazy and make her stomach get tight the way that Bryant did. Paul stood back to look at her, and she felt her face start to burn. "Now I know what everyone has been talking about," Paul said, turning to Bryant, and smiling. Macy was embarrassed, but just when she wished the floor would open up and swallow her, Bryant came to her side.

"Sorry about him," he explained to Macy, "Paul says the first thing that pops into his head, without thinking sometimes. Don't be embarrassed."

"Well it's not a lie," Paul said. "She's hot, you lucky dog."

Bryant rolled his eyes. "Macy, are you going to be alright staying here with my asshole brother? I promise I won't take any longer than I have to." She shook her head to say yes. She'd be fine. He slid his hand through her hair, stopping at the nape of her neck to pull her in for a kiss. It wasn't just a little peck, either. His tongue played with her lips until she opened for him. His kiss was deep and passionate as if he was telling her his feelings for her without words.

By the time he pulled away, Macy's mind was in a fog. He whispered, "When I get back we can talk some more, but I don't want you to leave. Okay?" His lips touched hers once more, quickly, leaving Macy wanting more.

"And you," his tone changed as he addressed Paul, "behave yourself." He pointed to his brother. Paul made the sign of the cross over his heart.

After Bryant left, Paul sat down in a big armchair. Macy could feel his eyes on her, making her uncomfortable again. When she got nervous, she started talking to try to fill the silence. "So, Bryant tells me you're a fireman—that must be a hard job, do you like it?"

"I like it, sure. But I want to know is why Bryant hasn't said anything about you. The other night I heard about the two big guys that were after you, and then my brother helped sneak you out of our pub, and now here you are living with him."

"I—" she stammered, "I'm not living here. I'm just staying until it's safe to go back to my apartment."

"What kind of trouble are you in or do you have a rich ex somewhere, stalking you?"

Macy laughed. *Yeah, right, a rich ex that wanted to stalk me*, "No, I don't have a rich ex or any ex for that matter. I'm a reporter, and I'm working on a story that somebody doesn't want me to write. I was poking around somewhere, and now I have a couple of hired thugs following me. They broke into my apartment earlier tonight. Bryant has been helping me."

Paul grinned, "And yet, somehow, after watching him kiss you, I feel like there's more to it than that.".

Macy wasn't smiling back at him. "Not that I have to explain anything to you, but when I met your brother I was not looking for a boyfriend. The night I asked for his help, all I wanted to do was to sneak out the back door. He insisted on taking me home, because, as he claimed, he didn't want me waiting for the bus or walking around the city wearing Angela's skimpy dress."

Paul nodded his eyes far away as if picturing Macy in Angela dress. Macy continued, "I didn't even want Bryant to know where I lived, so I asked him to drop me off a few blocks away from my apartment, but one of my heels, or rather, Angela's heels, got stuck in the sidewalk and I twisted my ankle. Bryant carried me home and took care of me."

"My brother is definitely the kind of guy who would help a woman in need. However, I'm sure you must have given him some indication that you were interested, somewhere along the way. Like that kiss in the pub, for instance."

"That kiss was because I didn't want those men who were following me to recognize me, and... Well, maybe because I wanted to."

Paul smiled, "There you go, now was that so hard to admit?"

"Yes," she said. Paul was now laughing at her, which made her more frustrated. "I'm trying to climb this endless ladder at work. That's why I'm working on this story in the first place, and I told your brother I didn't have the time to put into a relationship."

"And you thought that would deter him?"

"Yes, because lots of guys don't want a relationship at all, much less play second fiddle to a woman's career. Bryant didn't care because he just kept showing up. The night after he carried me home, he brought me dinner. He didn't know what I would like, so he brought this whole variety of fast food." Macy smiled as she remembered that evening.

"That sounds like him. So, what's this story you're working on that's got these guys out to get you?"

"I really don't want to put anyone else in danger. I've already put your brother and my neighbor right in the middle of this."

Paul laughed again. "Nobody puts Bryant anywhere that he doesn't want to be. Now tell me why I'm here sitting with you while my brother fixes your broken door."

Macy took a deep breath and told Paul about the missing girls, and about how her investigation must be on the right track since the two men were following her. She told him about her conversation with Mr. Smith, and her search for the owners that had led to the weird, shifting trail of corporate ownership. She even mentioned that she had a friend who was sending surveillance video to her. Paul asked what clubs were involved, and he said he recognized many of the ones she mentioned. She went to her bag and pulled out her computer.

Bryant arrived at Macy's place in record time, but already there were police on the scene. Before he left home, he'd gathered the tools he would need to fix her door. Now he pulled these from the front seat and walked towards her building. He knew Mark and two of his men would already be inside. The door to her building was open, so Bryant went straight to the elevators and up to Macy's floor. He found the door wasn't kicked in—it lay in pieces on her floor. He saw that Mrs. Wilkins's door had damage also, though not as bad as Macy's had. There was a cop standing in Macy's doorway, and he stopped Bryant from entering the crime scene.

"I'm meeting Detective Bobby Hernandez," he said. "Bryant O'Shea." The officer nodded, then called over his shoulder, "Bobby, there's a guy here to see you."

"If its Bryant O'Shea, let him in," came a voice from the other room.

Bryant watched as a man, shorter than himself by a few inches, walked out of Macy's bedroom. Right away, Bryant got an uncomfortable feeling. He didn't like to think that Bobby had been in there going through Macy's personal things. Not that Bryant himself hadn't had his hands in her panty drawer—with permission, of course.

Bobby pulled one of his gloves off and shook Bryant's hand. Bobby was of Latin descent, with dark hair and a mustache and goatee. He was broad across the chest, so Bryant knew he was no slacker, and surely, he knew his way around a gym. Bryant couldn't help sizing him up.

"When Macy called me at home tonight, I thought—" Bobby stopped and, looking at Bryant, changed his statement. "I never thought it would be for something like this." He moved his hand to gesture to the mess in Macy's living room.

Bryant asked Bobby, "You know what this is all about, don't you?"

Bobby responded, "Macy told me you would be here, but she didn't say who you are. What do you know about this?"

"I'm Macy's boyfriend," he said. Bryant watched Bobby's face closely to see his reaction.

"Really? Because she's never mentioned you before." Clearly, Bobby was sizing Bryant up too. "I guess that's why she declined my invitation to dinner when I asked."

"Yeah, she told me about drinks and lunch, or whatever you two worked out." He didn't want to get into a pissing match with the guy, because he was going to need Bobby's help to keep Macy safe. "You helped her with information about the—" Bryant looked around and said quietly, "—the missing girls."

Bobby frowned, "What does that have to do with this?"

"Everything," Bryant told him what had happened over the past few days—the men following Macy, the previous attempt to get into her building, the worry that they knew where she worked.

"Shit," Bobby said, "I would never have let her look at those case files if I thought it would put her in any danger. I didn't think anything would come of it when she asked. I thought what could be the harm? Although it's funny, my superiors weren't happy when I requested the surveillance tapes from the nightclubs. My boss said to leave it alone because the force had better things to worry about than some runaway girls. I should have told her no, but who can say no to

Macy Greene?" Bryant saw the lust in the other man's eyes when he said her name. He knew exactly how Bobby felt because he felt that way each time he thought about Macy.

Bryant asked, "What can I do to keep her safe?"

"It's a good thing she wasn't here when they came looking for her. She definitely can't stay here," Bobby said.

Duh, Bryant thought. "She's staying with me," he said. "I knew it wasn't safe for her here. I've already tried to talk her out of going any further with her investigation, but as you can imagine, that was a no-go."

"Yeah, Macy's more than a little headstrong," Bobby said. Bryant knew all too well. He'd known that within an hour of meeting her.

Though Bryant wanted to get back to Macy, he and Bobby talked for about an hour while the crime scene people finished photographing her apartment and lifting samples for fingerprints. Only once, they'd finished could Bryant replace Macy's door and fix Mrs. Wilkins's door. He was away from Macy for much longer than he expected or wanted to be, even though he knew she was safe with his brother.

Bryant still wanted to finish talking to her about what had happened in bed. It wasn't going to be easy to make her understand why he couldn't just jump into a physical relationship with her, even though he wanted to.

He wanted their first time to be special, and he needed to know that Macy felt the same way about him as he did for her. As crazy as it sounded, he'd known since the moment she kissed him in the pub that she was different from any other woman he'd ever met. He'd known she should be his wife. He didn't know how he knew, but it felt right. He couldn't ignore his feelings for her. Bryant knew in his heart time would only make his feelings grow stronger. He knew nothing would change the way he felt about Macy Greene.

He needed an update. Why was it taking so long for them to bring her to him? He was growing impatient, and when he got angry, someone always had to pay. Picking up his phone, Mr. Smith dialed one of his goons. Answering on the second ring, he heard, "Yeah boss."

"Why is that reporter not in my office yet? I send two of you to get one weak woman, and days later, I still have nothing. I am not a patient man." The anticipation of what he had in mind for her excited him and made his blood rush south.

"We tossed her apartment so she would show up, but so far it's a no-go. The cops came and left, and now some guys are there fixing the door already—" he laughed, "—or what's left of the door, anyway."

"Well clearly your plan isn't working, now is it? Find her. Two days, that's all I'm giving you. And you don't want to know what I'll do to you if you disappoint me." He threw the phone onto the desk in frustration.

Once again, Mr. Smith's mind wandered to the reporter. He imagined having her tied up, so he could do as he pleased with her. "Yes, I'm going to enjoy the hell out of her," he sneered.

{15}

After dealing with the police and fixing the doors, Bryant rushed home. It was past midnight, and he knew that Macy would most likely be asleep already, but he hoped maybe she'd be awake so they could finish their conversation. He was exhausted, but the thought of Macy waited for him in his bed made his heart pound. He asked himself, "What the hell is wrong with you, O'Shea? You have a beautiful woman in your bed every night, willing to give you what you so desperately need, but you can't make yourself finish the job?" With all of the hard-ons, he'd had in the past few days, left no doubt how much he wanted her, so that wasn't the problem. This situation reminded him of a big firework display without a grand finale.

There wasn't a lot of traffic at that time of night, so it didn't take long for Bryant to notice one car, a few car-lengths back that seemed to be tailing him out of the city. He decided to test his theory, to see if the car was indeed following him. He took the next exit, pulling into a drive-thru, and ordered some food. He was hungry, but his main goal had been to see whether the car pulled into the restaurant too. As Bryant pulled around the side of the building to pick up his food, sure enough, there was the car that had been behind him. The car was parked off to the side and Bryant could see two men inside.

He decided to ask the men for directions so he could get close enough to see their faces. He would know if they were the same guys who'd been following Macy.

Bryant parked his truck next to the car and started eating his food. The men didn't move. Bryant looked over into their car, and sure enough, the one guy he could see was the same one who'd been in the pub, and who'd tried to get into Macy's building. Bryant smiled and rolled his window down. The men didn't look at him, so he tapped his horn to get their attention.

The man on the driver's side opened his window, "Yeah?"

Bryant asked in a sarcastic tone, "Sorry, I was wondering if I could get some directions. I noticed you were behind me, so I figured you might be familiar with the area."

The guy from the passenger seat leaned forward and said, "We thought you knew where you were going." The driver backhanded him to shut him up.

Bryant smiled. "I think you fellas might want to take a different route from here on out." He rolled up his window and backed out of his parking space. He left the fast food place, waiting to see whether the car would follow him. It didn't look like they did, but Bryant decided to take a long way home, just in case.

When he walked through his front door, Bryant saw his brother Paul sleeping on the couch, the remote control in his hand. Hearing the door open, Paul cracked open an eye, and then shut it again. Bryant didn't care if Paul stayed there, but he was going upstairs, to bed, with Macy. As Bryant kicked off his boots, Paul sat up and asked what time it was.

"It's after one now. It took longer than I thought at Macy's because they had the crime scene guys go over every inch of that place before they even let me touch the door."

"I have to go on shift at the firehouse in the morning. Is it alright if I just crash here?" Paul yawned and stretched.

"Sure. But remember we have a lady in the house, so keep your pants close at hand." Bryant went to the closet to get what his brother would need for the night.

"Yeah, I'll be out of here early, no problem." Paul stripped off his pants and shirt. Bryant threw him a pillow and a better blanket. Paul chuckled, "I knew you weren't sleeping on the couch when you have something like that upstairs in your bed. You, lucky bastard."

Bryant opened his bedroom door as quietly as he could, and then let his eyes adjust to the darkness. Yes, he was one lucky man. He moved to Macy's side of the bed. It was late, and she had work in the morning—as did he—but he could watch her sleep forever. Wanting to touch her cheek, he used one finger to slide her hair out of her face gently. He whispered, "I think I'm in love with you, Macy Greene." She seemed to mumble something, but he couldn't make out what she said.

Walking to his side of the bed, he quietly stripped out of his clothes and slipped under the covers just as she rolled over to face him. She made a little smacking sound with her lips that made him want to kiss her. Gliding a hand over her hip, he realized she wasn't wearing anything on her legs. His mind went wild, then her bare leg crossed over his, and she snuggled in close.

Bryant had to remind himself to breathe, waiting to see what she would do next. A raspy "Mumm" came from Macy's direction, and Bryant went instantly hard. He didn't know if she was still asleep or not. Then her hand found his cock as if she knew it would be ready for her.

"Macy," he whispered.

Again, Macy made the little sound, "Mumm," almost as if she was answering him.

He asked, "Macy, what are you doing?"

"Dreaming," she murmured. "A really good dream… Shh, don't wake him."

"Who Macy, who don't you want to wake?" Bryant asked in a desperate whisper.

"Bryant. Don't wake him up. I want to play some more." Her tiny hand slid into his boxers. Bryant squeezed his eyes tightly closed, trying to stay still as her hand fondled him. He lifted his hips and adjusted his leg to give her better access to his body. She made that same little humming noise again, and Bryant thought he might lose it. Macy did things to him that she didn't even realize.

His hands itched to touch her, but he still wasn't sure if she was awake or not. He moved to put his mouth to hers, and when she kissed him back, his body took over. Knowing he couldn't resist her, he gave in to his deepest need for her. His hands pushed at the t-shirt she wore, sliding it up over her ribs until he caressed her breast. Letting his fingers play with her nipples, he lightly pinched and then tugged at them. Her moans told him she liked what he was doing, and the other little sounds she started to make turned him inside out.

Bryant rolled her onto her back and kissed her with everything he had. Then he let his mouth work its way down her body, sucking on her skin as she'd done to him, nibbling his way to her breast. Taking one of her nipples in his mouth, he circled her puckered peak with his tongue. He could stay there all night.

"Yes, please, I need more," she said, as her back arched up to meet him.

"I know you do. I don't plan to stop this time. I need you." There was nothing that was going to stop him this time.

"God, I'm so sorry for pulling Bryant off his path, but I'm weak." Macy didn't sound sorry at all.

Bryant chuckled as he moved southward, but Macy stopped him with her urgent tugging at him. He went willingly, moving on top of her. He looked down at her and confessed, "I think I'm falling for you, Macy." Sliding his boxers off, he reached for a condom, but Macy stopped him when she said, "I'm on birth control. And I've never done it without a—" He kissed her words away.

"Oh, God, Macy, I haven't either." The thought of really feeling her, all of her, was almost too much for him. "Are you sure, Macy?" He wanted to give her a chance to change her mind.

"Yes." She trusted him to be the first to take her without protection. She would be his first in that way, too.

With their bodies aligned, she was ready for him to enter her. Watching Macy as he pushed inside her was the most amazing thing he'd ever seen. Her eyes closed, and the sounds she made had him fighting the overwhelming desire for immediate release. Her legs opened wider, allowing him to sink deeper inside of her. He held tight to the sheets over her head as he felt her move under him. He knew she wanted him to move and thrust, but he was barely holding on by a thread.

"Give me a minute," he said, "I don't want this to be over before it begins. Being inside of you, skin to skin like this, you have no idea how close I am." He slowly started to move, just a steady pace at first, not trusting himself to kiss her.

Macy's hands went to his ass, and she slapped him. The sting sent a jolt through him, and he couldn't hold back any longer. His mouth smashed into hers, and he moved deeper and harder inside her. He held on until he felt her muscles starting to convulse around him. Looking down and watching Macy come, he felt his balls draw tight as his release hit hard. The pleasure was like nothing he'd ever felt before.

Kissing her tenderly, he said, "You know what this means, don't you?" He chuckled.

"What?" Macy asked.

"I have to marry you now." He enjoyed her little gasp. "It's true. I have to make an honest woman out of you because I don't want people talking." He was just messing with her, but the thought of having Macy in his life was already there.

Macy laughed. "And just who are these people who are going to be talking about me?"

"My family. You don't know the powers of my mother. She'll know just by looking at me that we've already done the deed."

"The deed. You mean to say your mother will know that I pulled you to the dark side—totally against your will, of course."

"Well of course," he said, their bodies still entwined.

She smacked his ass again, and his body started to harden. He hadn't withdrawn from her, and he was ready to take her once more. Soon it would be time for them to start their days, but all he wanted to do was stay in bed with Macy and make love to her over and over again.

"Call in sick tomorrow and spend the day with me," he said as he started to move inside her.

"I can't."

"It's almost time to get up." He was moving faster now. She didn't answer this time, because she was too involved in their lovemaking. That was fine with him—her silence gave him a chance to claim her mouth. As their tongues mingled, she started making those little sounds of pleasure that drove him crazy. Moving faster now, he felt her getting close. He reached down to find her sensitive spot. She came with a moan loud enough to wake his brother downstairs. Bryant had to cover her mouth with a kiss to muffle the sound. He knew that if Paul heard their lovemaking, Bryant would never hear the end of it.

"Shh, baby, you don't want to wake my brother on the couch." He wanted her to know they weren't alone.

Macy's eyes widened, and she slapped a hand over her mouth as she realized they weren't alone in the house. "Oh my God, why didn't you tell me that Paul's still downstairs?" she buried her face in his chest, embarrassed.

"You didn't give me much of a chance to tell you. I was a little preoccupied, as you recall. Paul will be gone soon—he's going on shift at the firehouse today. If you call in sick, we could both stay in bed all morning."

"You can't call in either, though. You're the boss." Macy knew Bryant didn't take off often.

"I can call in," he grinned, "because I'm the boss." Just then, they heard the front door close. Macy hid her face, thinking Paul probably had heard her moans. "I told you I'm going to have to marry you, right?" Bryant asked.

Macy reached up to touch Bryant's face, "I don't want you to have to do any such thing."

"Believe me, sweetheart, I don't do anything I don't want to." He kissed her forehead.

"So, what you're saying is you don't want to marry me?" Her brow lifted to question his words.

"Ms. Greene, I do believe your investigative reporter side is showing. Are you asking me to marry you?"

"Oh... um... Well, no," she was tripping over her words.

Bryant laughed at her indecisiveness. He loved the way she seemed flabbergasted by his question. He wished he could see her face clearly. He knew she would be blushing. Kissing her, he said, "We need to clean up. Do you want to shower with me?"

"Well, that depends."

"On?"

"It depends on if you're done busting my chops? I know you were just trying to see how I would react, and I fell for it."

"Ah, but you're so cute when you get all flustered and don't know what to say. Now, how about that shower?" Bryant started to get off the bed as Macy came with him.

She stood and took his hand, towing him off the bed behind her. He went willingly, smacking her on her cute little tush.

Macy couldn't believe Bryant had made love to her, twice, and now she was thinking about calling in sick to work—something she'd never done before—to spend the day with him. Situations like these were why she didn't think she had time for a boyfriend. In a million years, she never would have thought that she'd take time off work to spend with a man. The thought of having him to herself all day did sound wonderful, and she planned to use that time wisely.

Once inside the shower, he pinned her against the wall, kissing her until she couldn't think straight. He couldn't possibly want her again so soon after they'd just made love twice. But apparently, she was wrong, because that was exactly what Bryant had in mind.

Macy grabbed his shoulders as he lifted her, wrapping her legs around his waist. He whispered in her ear that she could make as much noise as she wanted to—he wanted to hear her. With the things he did to her body, she couldn't have stopped the noises of pleasure from escaping her lips even if she'd tried. The way he touched his lips, and hands to her skin made every nerve in her body tingle.

She held tightly to his broad shoulders as he supported her weight, one hand on the wall behind her. Her legs clenched tight around him as she reached her peak once more. This time she heard Bryant grunt and opened her eyes just in time to see his jaw and neck tighten. He looked like he was in agony, but she knew it wasn't pain he was feeling. The pleasure made him clench his teeth.

When he opened his eyes, he said, "Now that the dam has broken, I don't think I'll ever be able to get enough of you." She kissed his jaw, then his lips, using very soft touches.

"Macy, do you remember what I said earlier?"

"You said a lot of things. Can you be a little more specific?"

"You know—when I said that I think I'm falling for you. Actually, I think I was wrong. I think I already fell, and hard. I don't want to scare you, but I love you, Macy."

She blinked a couple of times as if she couldn't have heard him right. "Bryant, how could you possibly know that you love me? You don't even really know me." Macy couldn't believe what he was saying. She watched him as he chose his next words.

Taking her hand, he put it over his heart and said, "I feel it in here, Macy. It's something I've never felt before for any other woman. I've never said those words to anyone else except family."

172

"Bryant, I'm sorry, but I can't say those words back to you. It's too soon for me. All I know is that I like being with you and that I'm willing to call in sick to spend the day with you. That is something I've never done before. That alone tells me I have very strong feelings for you, but love, I—"

Bryant kissed her words away. He knew that she cared for him, and that was good enough for him. It was just going to take her more time to get comfortable with things, and that was all right with him. He just wanted her to know how he felt about her.

When he released her lips, he said, "I don't want you to feel pressure to say it back to me. I understand it might take a little longer for you to feel the same, but I needed you to know how I feel." Not wanting their conversation to become too serious, he picked up the soap and started to wash her. Moving his hands over her body did crazy things to him. No one had ever had such a pull over him before.

Macy was the first woman he'd had in his bed, and the first he'd slept with all night. He found that he slept better with her there, underneath the covers with her warm body pressed against his. There were many firsts with Macy. She was different from any woman, and it wasn't lost on him that Macy felt comfortable enough to have sex with him without protection. Just the feel of her body moving with his and nothing in between, making love to Macy without any restriction was amazing.

They both called in sick—Macy calling Mr. Sisco and Bryant calling his foreman, who owed him a day anyway. They climbed back into bed together and fell fast asleep. After being awake for over twenty-four hours, then making love to Macy three times, as soon as Bryant's head touched his pillow, he was out.

They sat in the car, waiting across the street from the newspaper office, watching for Macy Greene to come to her building. The men thought it would be easy—when she came to work they'd grab her. Except Macy never showed. Nothing went the way they thought it would where this woman was concerned.

Mr. Smith was becoming very unhappy with them, and when he wasn't happy, bad things happened. They only had one more day to bring her to him before things would get ugly, and Daniel knew he wasn't going let it be his ass on the line. If the idiot next to him hadn't opened his mouth, they could have followed the guy home last night, and they probably would have found her with him. Instead, the dumbass had told him, to his face, that they'd been following him. After that, Daniel had told Henry to keep his mouth shut. Since then, Daniel had been enjoying their stakeout in silence, except for the fact that they still hadn't brought Macy Greene to the boss.

He would watch the office building all day if he needed to, waiting until tomorrow would be cutting it too close. Daniel knew exactly what Mr. Smith was capable of because he had seen him in action before, leaving women, girls, men, and even young boys close to death. In the back of his mind, Daniel knew his boss would like nothing better than to make him someone's bitch—maybe even his bitch. His boss was one sick son-of-a-bitch. Daniel knew better than to think that with his strength, he could overpower the other goons that Mr. Smith had working for him. They would drug him, as they did to everyone Mr. Smith wanted to become part of his sick world. Then, Daniel would wake up strapped down and tied up, to be a plaything for anyone who paid enough money to get their jollies. Daniel felt sweat running down his neck. He cranked his head to the side, letting his neck crack, releasing some of the tension that was building there.

He had to find Macy Greene, and soon.

{16}

Cracking open one eye, Macy could see daylight through the blinds. Getting her bearings, she took a deep breath and turned to see Bryant still fast asleep. His body lay stretched out before her, with the covers only over his feet. He must have gotten hot and kicked them off. This gave her a chance to take in every inch of the view. Her eyes tracked over his jaw with its reddish growth that she wanted to feel. Then she gazed at his chest, looking at the hair that spread across his pecs—also a reddish color, and very soft. She knew this because her cheek had pressed against it many times.

She didn't want to wake him, or for him to roll over and end her appreciative exploration. Using just the tip of her finger, she touched the small, flat disc of his nipple, watching it rise. She smiled as she moved to the other one, liking the way his nipples reacted to her touch. Bryant didn't move. Apparently, he was a deep sleeper, which encouraged her to continue. Her gaze followed the happy trail of hair that went right down the center of his well-defined ab muscles. Even in sleep, she could see his six-pack.

When her eyes swept over his penis, she could see it growing, though she hadn't even touched him there yet. Macy let her finger glide down his happy trail and into his pubic hair. Bryant shifted in the bed. Macy leaned over and put a kiss on the head of his member and Bryant stirred again. She started gliding her tongue around the crown, then down his shaft. Her movement made him murmur her name. Taking him deep into her mouth, she looked up and watched as his hands came to caress her face. As she started to really work him, his hands moved to her hair, tangling his fingers in it so he could hold her to him.

"Damn Baby, that feels so good, if this is what it's like waking up with you, then I'm all for it."

Macy giggled with him still in her mouth. The vibration of her laughter drove him crazy. He pulled her up, so they were eye-to-eye again. "Hey! I wasn't finished with you." She'd have to remember that giggling thing and do it again next time.

"I created a little sex pistol," Bryant laughed. "I've never had sex four times in less than twenty-four hours."

Again, Macy giggled, "You started it by hopping into the shower with me." She aligned her body so she could sink down onto him. When she did, the talking ended, and Bryant took her hips in hand moving her at the pace he wanted. Macy didn't care what the pace was—in that position he went deep, and the sensation was exquisite. Her head fell back as the pleasure felt so good.

She started to move faster, and Bryant watched her as his hands went to cup her bouncing breasts. When she saw him close his eyes and toss his head back, Macy knew he was close. As if, he knew she needed more, his free hand reached between her legs and sent her flying along with him.

When they had finished, Bryant pulled her down onto his chest and wrapped his arms tightly around her body. A few minutes later, after he'd caught his breath, Bryant said, "I created a monster, a beautiful, sexy monster."

"I couldn't help myself," Macy said. "I woke up and saw you spread out on the bed with only your feet covered. I just had to touch you, and when you didn't wake up right away, I wanted to have some fun." Macy looked up at him.

"Are you taking advantage of me already? Just remember, I'll get my turn too. You know what they say about payback, don't you?" He moved his brows up and down.

"It's a bitch," she said, laughing. She was sure that payback would be quite pleasurable.

He quickly flipped her over so that he was on top. Taking her lips, he kissed her softly, and then asked, "What would you like to do today, my little Sex Pistol?"

"Sex Pistol? Mmm…Well, first I want to hear about what happened last night at my apartment, and if they took anything."

Bryant told her he didn't think anything was missing. He explained how the men had just made a mess of her place—knocking over furniture, pulling books from shelves, throwing clothes from the dresser. Bryant shared some of the conversation he had with her friend Bobby Hernandez. He told her how he'd had to replace her door entirely because there hadn't been anything left to fix. "I had to fix Mrs. Wilkins's door too."

"Oh no! Did they hurt her? Please tell me she's alright." Macy closed her eyes because she didn't want to hear something bad had happened to her neighbor.

"No, she's fine and feisty as ever. She yelled through the door to say she was calling the police, and that's why I think they hit her door. But as crazy as she is, she told them to go ahead and kick it down because she had her shotgun aimed and ready to blast the first S.O.B. that came through her door."

"That sounds like Mrs. Wilkins. She may be old, but she doesn't take crap from anybody. I guess, I should go over to the apartment and clean up."

Was she crazy? "Macy, no, you can't go anywhere near your place, because I know for a fact that they're watching your apartment. Those two assholes tried to follow me home last night." He shook his head at the thought of how stupid those two guys were.

Macy questioned, "Well if they know I'm here, then don't we need to go?"

"No, I ditched them." He told her what happened in the drive-thru parking lot.

"How stupid can they be?"

"Macy this lets me know they aren't just trying to scare you. I think they want to make you disappear, like the other girls. I know you're not backing down from investigating your story, but please be careful. I don't want you to go anywhere by yourself. Okay?" He hated the thought of something happening to her.

"But I still have to do my job. If I let them control what I do and when I do it, then I'm letting them win. Don't you see, they'll get what they want by either silencing me or abducting me. In the end, it's the same thing because they would succeed."

"Look, I know. All I'm asking is that you be careful. I couldn't bear it if anything happened to you. I mean, come on, I just found you, and I don't plan on losing you."

"Alright, I won't take any unnecessary risks. I'll watch out for the two men. I can even wear a disguise, you know, tuck my hair into a hat or something. Or dress like Angela every day." Bryant didn't want her dressing like Angela and walking around the city. He kissed the crease in her brow, hoping to ease the tension that showed there.

"So, tell me, how did things go with my brother while I was away? What did you guys do?"

Macy looked at Bryant as if all his marbles had just rolled out of his head. "What do you mean, what did I do with your brother? Because I didn't do anything."

Bryant laughed at her righteousness. He wasn't accusing her of any wrongdoing, but damn, she was so cute when she stood her ground. "No, Honey, I wasn't saying anything inappropriate happened. I was just asking what you guys did while he was here."

"Oh, well…we talked… about you and then we talked about me staying here with you… Hm…Then we looked over the nightclub footage that Bobby sent me. Paul was very helpful, because he had been to some of the clubs, both at night as a patron, and again in the daytime, to do the fire inspections. So, he could tell me a lot about how some of the clubs were laid out."

"I'm sorry I couldn't help with that. I'd still like to see the tapes." He wanted to help her in any way he could.

"You don't want me to work on the one day when I called in sick, do you?"

"I don't mind what we do. I just wanted to spend the day with you. If you still want to go and check out the clubs as we planned, I'd be fine with that too. While we're out I'll take you to lunch and show you some of my favorite buildings that I've remodeled—that is if you want to see them."

"I'd love to do that," Macy said, and with that, they got out of bed and began to get dressed.

Bryant showed Macy some of the old houses he'd done first. They passed a gingerbread Victorian with brightly colored trim. Bryant told her that he hadn't chosen the paint colors, but with the crazy hues, Macy could appreciate the amazing detail. It reminded her of the house he was fixing up for himself.

Then he wanted to show Macy an office building where he'd worked. He parked the truck this time so that he could take her inside. Astonished by the grand entryway, Macy was speechless. The reception area had two tiers, joined by a beautiful staircase that appeared to be floating in mid-air. The workmanship on the railing had Macy gasping. Drawn to it like a magnet, Macy forgot anyone was even watching her as she went to the staircase and began gliding her hand over the wood, much as Bryant had seen her do at his house.

Her eyes studied the carvings in the wood, and then she looked up at Bryant in amazement. He smiled because he liked looking at Macy when she didn't think anyone was watching her. He knew he was showing off a bit by bringing her here, to one of his best accomplishments, but he knew Macy shared his fascination with making old things new again. He had seen it when she looked around his house.

"Bryant, have you thought of doing something like this at your house, maybe not as grand, but something similar?" He had, but he wanted her to think it was her idea.

"I haven't given it much thought, but yeah, I can see it. I'll sketch something out and see if you like it."

"You can do that? Just sketch something and then make it happen?" She looked at him with amazement.

Again, Bryant smiled, because he loved the twinkle in her eyes and the way she looked at him.

"Why are you looking at me like that?" She smiled at him quizzically, and he swore his heart skipped a beat.

"Because I can, and because I enjoy watching you look at wood. You have this way of feeling its essence, the spirit of the wood. I can see it when you run your hand over it. You did the same thing at my house, on the banister."

"I like how it feels under my hand. This is amazing work. No, amazing isn't a good enough word, maybe astonishing?" She walked up the stairs to the top, then back down again, without letting go of the railing.

"Well, if you keep handing me compliments like that I'm going to get a big head." She gave him a wicked smile that told him she'd found the hidden meaning in his words that he hadn't intended. He said her name in warning, "Macy."

She walked to him, lifting her arms, and putting them around his neck. "What?"

"You know what," playfully chastised her. He encased her in his arms. Feeling her close to him just felt right in every fiber of his being. They fit perfectly together, and he didn't want anything to come between them. Taking one hand, he cupped her face. "You ready to get something to eat?" That wasn't what he wanted to say, but it was a safe choice of words.

"I guess I could be persuaded to leave this beautiful staircase. You are so talented, to be able to see something like this in your head." Macy turned to see the railing one more time as she added, "and then make it so that others can enjoy it too. I bet the building's owner went crazy over this. I hope he paid you well."

"I get by alright," he said, wrapping his arm around her shoulder leading them toward the door.

While they were at lunch, Bryant asked if Macy wanted to meet his uncle. He promised it wouldn't be anything formal— they'd talk with him for a few minutes. He didn't want her to feel obligated to meet his family, but not only did Macy agree to meet with Uncle Joe, but she also said that, if she could, she'd like to speak with him in private.

Macy didn't know how Bryant would handle her request, but she had a few questions that she couldn't talk to him about, not that she wanted to talk about personal matters with a complete stranger. Bryant's uncle would clear up a few things for her.

Once they were back in the truck, Macy started to feel nervous. They quietly drove into the city. Every so often, she felt Bryant looking over at her. She didn't want to look back, because she didn't want him to see how uncomfortable she was becoming. Looking out the window, she asked, "So what do I call your uncle, Father Joe, just Father, or Uncle Joe? Well… no… not Uncle Joe, that wouldn't feel right. I don't know…" her voice drifted off as if she was thinking to herself. She knew she was babbling, but that's how she always filled uncomfortable silences.

"Have you changed your mind about meeting my uncle? Because if you did, that's okay, just let me know. We don't need to do this today. We can do it some other time." He glanced over at her and then looked back at the road.

"No, I haven't changed my mind, it's just… I guess I'm nervous is all. I need to know how to address him. It's nice to meet you, Mr…Father… just-plain-Joe."

Bryant laughed. "Well, first of all, he's not all that formal. He doesn't demand to be called Father O'Shea. He always says he's a man first, and foremost. A godly man, of course, but a man nonetheless. He's pretty relaxed."

Macy said in a huff, "Well, that doesn't really help me decide what I should call him."

"Don't worry about it. I just want to introduce you to my uncle, that's all." He pulled into a parking lot of Our Lady of Mercy Catholic Church, turning off the engine. Taking her hand, he smiled, "It will be just fine, you'll see."

The church was very old looking as if it had stood there for hundreds of years. The red brick on the exterior was dull and rough, with stunning stained-glass windows that lined the side of the building. The structure was enormous, and Macy looked up to the white steeple. She almost tripped over her own feet and was glad when Bryant steadied her. They walked up the few steps to the two massive wooden doors. They must have weighed a hundred pounds each, but Bryant opened one with ease, and they entered the church. As Macy looked around, she noticed a tiny alcove that held a small stand. On the stand were rows of candles, many twinkling with firelight.

This was not Macy's first time in a Catholic church. As a child, she'd gone to church often, but after her grandfather died, her parents had stopped going.

Bryant took Macy's hand and led her to the front of the church, gesturing to the first pew on the right. "This is where we sit on Sunday. When you accepted my mother's offer to join us for Mass, I don't think you knew what you were getting yourself into." With a few more steps, they stood at the altar.

Macy didn't think they should be standing up there, and she kept glancing around as if someone might see them. "I don't think we should be up here. Isn't it like, holy or something?" She whispered so that no one could hear her.

Bryant smiled at her. "There is nothing wrong with us being up here. We aren't hurting anything. I just wanted to show you my church. This is where Uncle Joe will be standing on Sunday."

"Bryant, Sunday will not be the first time I've been to Mass. I just haven't been in a very long time."

A voice from behind them asked, "And why is that?"

They both turned to see a man in a priest's collar standing behind them. He looked a lot like Bryant. This must be Father O'Shea, who smiled now as he closed the distance to give Bryant a warm hug. "I'm surprised to see you here in the middle of a workday," he said. "And this lovely young lady must be Macy."

Macy extended her hand to shake. Uncle Joe took her hand in his and then placed the other hand on top, encasing Macy's hand. "It's good to meet you, Macy. I've heard so much about you."

Macy could feel her face heat up. Oh no, does he know I've taken Bryant to the dark side? She wondered.

"Come, let's go into my office where we can sit." They followed Bryant's uncle down a hallway that ran off to the side of the altar. They passed a few women seated at desks and Bryant greeted each one by name. Macy smiled and said hello as she passed. She could feel their eyes on her as she entered the office. When the door clicked shut behind them, she had the feeling of being sent to the principal's office.

Father Joe sat down behind his desk, and Macy took in the family resemblance. His hair was the first thing she noticed, although he was balding, it had that reddish hue as everyone she met in his family possessed. But it was his facial features—the color of his eyes that were the same blue-green as Bryant's, and the strong, handsome jawline—these showed that the men were related.

"So, Bryant, what brings you by?" Resting his hands on his desk, Father Joe looked only at his nephew.

"I wanted to show Macy the church and introduce you. As you already know, because you requested it." His uncle smiled.

"Yes, I guess I did ask that," turning to look at Macy, he said, "I don't think I've ever known Bryant so taken with anyone before. So of course, I wanted to meet you."

"It's nice to meet you too, um… what should I call you? Father Joe? Or would you prefer something else?"

"Whatever you're comfortable with, Father Joe, Uncle Joe, just Joe."

Once they'd spoken together for a while, Macy asked if she could speak to his uncle privately. Bryant left the office and shut the door. He was curious to know what she might have to say to Uncle Joe.

Macy wasn't sure how to say what she needed to ask. As Bryant's uncle patiently waited for her to speak her mind, Macy's thoughts rambled through her head.

"I asked to speak to you because Bryant has already expressed a feeling of love for me. Quite frankly, I don't understand how anyone in his right mind can say or feel that way after only knowing someone for a matter of days. I do like Bryant, and I enjoy spending time with him, but love? I don't know. It's too early to say. You know him far better than I do. What do you think?"

"I see, so he knows how he feels, and he wants you to know, although you might need more time to understand your feelings. There's nothing wrong with analyzing and thinking things through, Macy. Just like there's nothing wrong with the way, Bryant is handling the relationship. You're two different people. Bryant wants you to know that he's serious about you. He doesn't take things of this nature lightly."

"Yes, but, to be perfectly honest with you, it scares me sometimes how I feel as if I've known him for years when really we just met a few days ago."

"Bryant is an open book. Once he lets you in, it's with all that he has to give. It seems like he's chosen you, Macy, just give it time."

Macy didn't know what to say to that.

{17}

As much as Bryant wanted to know what Macy had discussed with his uncle, he wouldn't ask, and he knew his uncle would never say. Driving back to his house with Macy felt normal, and he liked how for the last couple of days, they'd gone into work together and come home together. On the one hand, he wanted her investigation to be over and for her to be out of any danger, but on the other, he wanted her to stay with him. He was deep in thought when Macy put her hand on his thigh. He looked over at her.

"You okay?" she asked.

"Yep, just thinking how much I like the way we drive to work together and home again."

It didn't escape Macy that he wanted her to stay with him, even after she was no longer in any danger. She wasn't ready to move in, although she did like staying with him. Macy knew she needed to tell him that their arrangement was only short-term. "I like it too, but Bryant, I don't want you to be disappointed when I move back into my apartment once this is all over."

"You know you don't have to. I like having you living with me." He took her hand in his.

"Bryant, you can't be thinking this through. Your mother would have a cow, and technically, it would be a sin. Not that we haven't already, you know, gone to the dark side and all, but I have to go back to my apartment when this is all over."

"You're not saying we—" he started, wondering if she was leaving him for good.

Macy quickly let him know that she was talking only about the living arrangements, not about their relationship because she was already in too deep to walk away from him.

It had been a long day, and when they got back to Bryant's house, they decided to have dinner in bed while watching a movie. Shortly after their movie started, Macy fell fast asleep. Bryant turned it off and snuggled up close to her, and that's all it took for him to slip into a deep sleep.

The next morning was normal, for once. Bryant's parents hadn't shown up, and neither Bryant nor Macy called in sick to work. They got ready for their day side-by-side in the bathroom, bumping into one another in the tight space, sometimes on purpose. Bryant combed his hair over Macy's head as she brushed her teeth.

Bryant left earlier than his usual time, to get Macy into work when she liked to get there. The ride into the city wasn't bad at that time of the morning. Bryant kissed her good-bye as she climbed out of his truck. He watched her go inside her building before he drove away. He couldn't stop thinking how easily he could get used to having her with him, although she'd made it clear she wasn't staying with him once the danger was over. He would have to work on that.

Macy went into her building, looking over her shoulder to see if she spotted the men who were after her, but she didn't see anything unusual. She knew she was starting to become paranoid, but she had promised Bryant that she would be careful. Making it to her desk, she released a deep breath and started her computer. The peace and quiet greeted her as it did every morning when she made it into work so early. This gave her time to work on the missing girl's cases without anyone looking over her shoulder.

She'd learned from Paul how the club was laid out, and where the private offices sat adjacent to the public area. Macy was trying to find space where they might keep the girls, but where a fire inspector wouldn't look. She'd looked over the tapes many times, but Macy never saw the girls leave the building—not that they couldn't have moved the girls the next morning. Macy was thinking this case was leaning toward human trafficking. She didn't think Mr. Smith would keep the girls on the premises for too long. He would have had to move them to a different location, somewhere with more privacy. Macy started to feel a tension headache coming on.

It wasn't long before other reporters came into the office and started moving around, so Macy had to put aside the case. She didn't want anyone to catch wind of her story. As the day went on, it turned out to be a very busy news day. One by one, the reporters left the office to cover stories. Macy wondered if she'd ever get her turn to work a big story. The only two people left in her row of cubicles were Billy, who was working on a story he'd covered yesterday and was on a tight deadline, and Macy.

When Mr. Sisco yelled for her, she went to his office. "Macy, I need you to go and cover the shooting on—here," he wrote an address on a piece on paper and handed it to her. "I want you to take Billy with you. I know he's on deadline, but I don't want you out in the field alone on your first big story."

Macy wasn't happy that she had to bring Billy along, and apparently, he didn't seem to like it either. Having his camera with him meant extra money for him if they used his shots, so he went, but complained the entire way.

They exited the building in a hurry, hoping to be the first to arrive on the scene. Macy didn't pay attention to anyone on the street. All she was thinking about was her first big story. When they reached the corner and stood to wait to cross the street, a black van darted around the corner, stopping right in front of them. Two men opened the side door and hauled Macy and her co-worker inside, throwing them to the floor. Macy felt pain shoot in her shoulder where she hit the wheel well. Billy started fighting with the two guys, who had just damaged his camera equipment. But he was no match for them.

With a chill, Macy realized these were the same guys who'd been after her. Her stomach turned, and she wanted to throw up. She knew this was going to be bad, and she began to pray. One of the men threw a punch connecting with Billy's face, knocked him unconscious. The bigger man, Daniel, smiled down at Macy.

"Well, Ms. Greene, it seems we met again. You know, you're a hard woman to get a hold of, but as you can see, what Mr. Smith wants, Mr. Smith gets."

Macy kept quiet, trying to breathe and not pass out. She couldn't think, because her brain wasn't cooperating with her. How was she going to get herself out of this mess? Could she send off a text without the men noticing? She might have been able to when they'd been fighting with Billy, but now Daniel and the other guy were sitting there looking at her. Her mind was racing and yet she couldn't make any sense of what to do.

When they pulled into the alley behind The Black Dragon, Macy knew that if she didn't get away from the men before they got her inside, then she was never going to leave the place alive. Daniel took her arm forcefully and dragged her in through the club's back door. She didn't see what they did with Billy. *Oh God*, she realized, *they'll kill him too, because of me.*

Daniel took Macy through another door, and suddenly she knew exactly where she was—outside Mr. Smith's office. She'd been in this hallway the night she spoke with the infamous owner of The

Black Dragon. The other goon came up behind her and dropped Billy's lifeless body on the floor so that his hands were free to knock.

"What is it?" His annoyed voice came through the door.

Daniel said, "Mr. Smith, I have what you wanted."

The door opened so fast it hit the wall, and there he stood, smiling at her. As pretty as his face was, Macy could now see the devil that lurked beneath the surface. His eyes raked disgustingly over her body, and she felt ill. He stepped back and said, "Daniel, bring our guest in and make her comfortable in the chair in front of my desk." He looked down at the man sprawled on the floor. "And who might this be?"

Henry shrugged and said, "He was with her."

Mr. Smith rubbed his hands together, "Bring him in too. This will be more fun with an audience."

Macy closed her eyes, trying to breathe and not to allow Mr. Smith's words to overwhelm her. She needed to stay calm and keep her wits if she was going to make it out of here alive. She told herself that she had to survive, and she planned to do everything in her power to do just that. So she could get back to Bryant.

Daniel tied Billy to a chair that was about five feet away from hers, but his chair faced Macy's side. She could see the way his body slumped over that he would have a massive headache when he woke up. Macy did a sad laugh at the thought because he might end up dead before that could happen.

"You find something amusing, Ms. Greene? Do share." Mr. Smith cooed as he stepped up and lifted her chin.

Macy turned her face away from his touch, as she said, "I was just thinking that my colleague is going to have a bitch of a headache
191

once he wakes up. Then I laughed because I thought well, that's if he wakes up at all."

Mr. Smith walked to his desk and sat down before saying, "Why, Ms. Greene, we don't kill people here. They are too valuable alive. But then again, they say there are things far worse than death."

Macy tried to show Mr. Smith she wasn't afraid when she asked, "So, are you going to tell me what you did with those girls?"

"Oh, I will do you one better." He pushed a buzzer on his phone, and a voice came over the speaker, "Yes, Mr. Smith."

"Send them up to me," he said. The line went dead.

Mr. Smith stood as a door behind his desk opened—a door that Macy hadn't noticed before when she was here. What Macy saw made her gasp. The six girls she had pictures of on her iPad walked through the doorway, but they didn't look the same. They had bruises everywhere as if someone had beaten them. None of them looked at her. Their eyes stayed cast downward, submissively. As each one dressed in very revealing, figure-hugging clothing. Macy knew these girl's lives would never be the same again. It made her sick, and she even tasted the vial as it threatened to come up.

"So, you see, Ms. Greene, they are alive. But look at what you've done to them?"

Macy said in a sharp tone, "What I did to them?"

"It's cause and effect. You caused trouble for me, by sticking your pretty little nose where it didn't belong."

Angrily she responded, "I was just trying to find out what happened to them."

"Yes, well, when you did that, they paid the price, Ms. Greene."

It was getting on her nerves, the way he kept saying her name. But looking at these girls, beaten and abused, her annoyance slipped away.

Macy squinted at him and clenched her teeth as she said, "By your hand, Mr. Smith, not mine." He smiled a cocky smile. Macy wanted to slap it off his face.

"Oh, how I do love the way you say my name. I think it might be time to wake up her friend and start teaching Ms. Greene what happens when I'm displeased." He pressed the button on the wall next to the door, which opened just long enough for the girls to file out.

Macy looked over at Billy just as Daniel threw a bucket of water on him. Immediately he came to and groaned, attempting to put his hand on his head. Then Billy realized he couldn't move. Looking at his hands tied to the chair, he started trying to get loose. He yelled, "What the hell is going on?"

"Well hello, Mr.—, what is your name?" Mr. Smith walked over to him.

Billy was pissed and displayed his anger, "I'm Billy Furst, who the fuck are you, and why am I tied to a chair?"

Mr. Smith laughed, "Well, Mr. Furst, it seems you were in the wrong place at the wrong time. Sorry to say your collateral damage."

Billy's eyes darted to Macy. She wanted to say how sorry she was for getting him into this. Instead, she spoke to Mr. Smith, "He has nothing to do with this. He doesn't even know what I was working on, so why don't you let him go?"

"Sorry, Ms. Greene, but I know you're much smarter than that, I can't allow him to go blabbing about what he's about to witness. It pleases me, having him here to see what I plan to do to you." He stood in front of Macy, putting his finger under her chin. "I have waited for you, and this day, with great anticipation. We will have so much fun together."

Macy whispered, "Somehow, I don't think we are going to have fun at all."

"Why Ms. Greene, have you ever considered being an exhibitionist? It can be very stimulating." He shifted his gaze to Billy. "I think your friend here would agree with me. Isn't that right, Mr. Furst?"

"Wait a minute. If you think for one second I want to watch you do whatever you're planning to do to her, you're sick." His eyes never looked in Macy's direction. He kept them on the man standing over Macy. "Listen here, your sick son of a bitch, you touch one hair on her, and I'll kill you for it if it's the last thing I do." Billy pulled on his restraints with no avail.

Mr. Smith laughed hard as if Billy's threat meant nothing. It was true—tied up and immobile, what could Billy possibly do? "Now Ms. Greene, if you would come with me." He gave her no choice. Grabbing her arm, he made her stand and forced her over to the corner of the room. Now she stood in the corner that Billy faced, and Macy knew what was coming next wasn't going to be good. "Give me your arms, Ms. Greene." When Macy hesitated, Mr. Smith slapped her hard across the face, knocking her glasses to the floor.

Macy saw dark spots crowding her vision. She tried to breathe, to avoid passing out. She did as he asked, presenting her arms to Mr. Smith, and that's when she heard Billy making a fuss. Mr. Smith continued to tie her hands above her head on something that looked as if it was a coat rack bolted to the wall. Like the hidden door, Macy hadn't noticed it last time she'd been in his office.

"Yes, this is just how I saw you in my mind—at my disposal, to do with as I please. I have to say, I like it quite a lot, Ms. Greene. When you were here the last time, something about you intrigued me. You're like my little librarian, with those glasses." His finger ran down the front of her blouse in between her breasts. He hooked it into the top button, and then pulled until the button gave way. He did the same to each button until her blouse was completely open.

Macy didn't dare look over at Billy. She closed her eyes, trying to think of anything but what was about to happen. She was wearing a lace bra, and Macy knew it would be the next thing ripped away. Then her breasts would be exposed to everyone. Opening her eyes just in time to see Mr. Smith holding a pair of scissors, she squinted as he opened and closed the blades for her to see.

"I think it's time to open my present," Mr. Smith announced as he walked toward her. Billy again threw a fit, and Daniel punched him with his meaty fist, knocking Billy's head almost off his shoulders.

She watched as he slid the scissors between her breasts and cut her bra. This time Macy took the chance and glanced over at Billy, and she saw his head turned to the side with his eyes closed as if he wouldn't watch what was about to happen, and that was just as well.

It was almost quitting time, and as Bryant cleaned up materials and put tools away, he got an uncomfortable feeling. Pulling out his phone, he dialed Macy's cell. The call went straight to voicemail. That was odd, but her phone could have died without her noticing. Putting his phone away, because he would be seeing her soon anyway, he went on cleaning up the site.

After a half hour, he still couldn't shake the feeling that something was wrong, so Bryant called her again. Again, it went straight to voicemail. This time he left a message, asking her to call him as soon as she could. He decided he'd leave early and go to the newspaper office. He would feel better once he saw her and knew she was safe. Then he could put the uneasy feeling to rest.

He had to park a block and half away from her building, and as he walked the distance to the office, the feeling in his stomach got tighter. The last half-block he ran, and once inside the building, he rushed past security and up to her floor. If he found her sitting at her desk, he would have scared the crap out of himself for nothing, but he'd be happy. Running through the doorway, he saw people swiftly moving about, and everyone was talking at once. Bryant spotted a man that looked to be in charge. Bryant stepped up to the man, "Hi, I'm looking for Macy."

"Aren't we all? Macy and Billy went out on a story hours ago, and no one has seen them since. Mr. Sisco, our boss, has tried both their cell phones and got nothing." The man Bryant was talking to held out his hand, "I'm William Van Houten, and I work with Macy." They shook hands. "Today was one of those days where there was more news than we could report. Mr. Sisco didn't want to send Macy out in the field alone for her first big story, so he sent Billy along with her. When we realized they were gone longer than they should, we sent someone down to check if they ever made it to the site, it turns out they never did. We have no idea where they could have gone."

Bryant had an idea, but he couldn't barge into The Black Dragon without proof. Right away he asked, "Did you call the police?

"No, they won't do anything for forty-eight hours." That answer wasn't good enough for Bryant. With that, he turned and pulled out his phone. He knew of one cop in the city that would do something the instant he found out Macy was missing.

Bobby was out in the field, so Bryant left a message for him to call back as soon as he got the message. He told him that Macy was missing. After Bryant hung up with the detective's voice mail, Bryant called his friend from the electronics store where he'd bought all of Macy's spy gear. He was hoping Macy had the pen with her because he remembered his friend explaining everything it did.

"Hello, Bryant, what can I do for you?" It figured that Keven would know who was calling. He was the tech guy after all.

"Keven this is really important. That pen you sold me—can it track where the person who has it?"

Keven hesitated before he said, "Um, yeah, if you turn that feature on, why?"

Bryant was quick to say, "Because my girlfriend is missing, and I think I know where she is, but I can't just go busting down the doors until I know for sure that she's in there."

Keven was thinking off the cuff, "If she didn't activate it… Well, wait, I should be able to do it from here. I have the serial number on file. Hold on a sec, and I'll see what I can do."

Bryant yelled, "Wait! Keven, is there any way of hearing what that pen is recording right now?"

"I can have a transmitter hooked to the pen. You must be within a hundred feet. Do you want me to set that up too while I'm at it?"

"Yes. When can I get that? I need it like now. This could be the difference between life and death."

"Okay, I'm on it. Do you want me to bring it to you?"

"That would be great, Keven. I owe you big time for this."

The next phone call Bryant made was to his father.

{18}

Bryant looked at the screen on his phone. The little green circle stayed in the same spot, meaning Macy, or the pen wasn't moving. Either way, Bryant knew where he was going, and when he got there, Bryant would need all the help he could get. When he spoke to his father and told him what was happening, Cadman had told Bryant not to worry—he'd take care of getting the help they needed.

When Cadman got off the phone with Bryant, he called the pub and told Mack to shut it down because Bryant needed help, not only did his family pull together, but all of the customers came too. The nightclub wasn't far from the pub, so the mob marched straight to The Black Dragon's front door.

Cadman had also called his boys in the fire department and told them that Bryant needed them. Any of the off-duty men left with Paul and came to help. Paul then called his brothers and Uncle Joe to tell them that Macy was missing and most likely was being held at The Black Dragon so that they were on their way to help too.

When Bryant pulled up in front of the club, he double-parked. He didn't give a rat's ass about his truck getting towed. When he got out, he realized that all of the people standing out front were people he knew—people from the pub, old and young, and firefighters, and friends of his brothers. When they saw Bryant the crowd parted, he saw his father standing at the door, talking to the bouncer showing him his chief shield from the fire department.

"Sorry, but I'm afraid you're going to have to let us in. This is a surprise fire inspection." Cadman barely had shown the guy his fire chief badge before he was moving through the doorway. Once the bouncer had opened the little gate that barred the doorway, everyone started to pile into the nightclub.

"Hey! You all can't be with the fire department. What the hell— this one's a priest!" he protested and tried to stop the crowd from moving past him, but everyone pushed their way beyond him. Bryant was right behind his father, with his two brothers, Paul, and Mack close by his side. Bryant put in an earpiece. He knew he was close, and that Macy was still alive because he could now hear what was happening to her. Anguish stabbed through his heart as he listened to the torturing sounds that Macy was enduring. He had to find her, and fast.

Behind the office door, Macy was losing all hope she would ever see Bryant again, but the thought of him was the only thing keeping her going. A sharp pain shot through her arms and shoulders from hanging on the hook for hours. She could taste blood in her mouth, and one of her eyes was swollen shut. Blood caked down her face from the deep gash on her cheek. At that point, she no longer cared that she hung there naked. Mr. Smith had stripped her of her dignity hours ago. She no longer felt the welts he'd given her from whipping her with the riding crop. Macy tried her best not to react when he struck her had only resulted in him hitting her harder until the sounds escaped her lips of their own accord. She felt she was losing consciousness from the severe pain. It was a dream-like state, where thoughts went in and out of her mind.

When Macy knew she couldn't take much more, she closed her eyes and thought about marrying Bryant. She kept her mind on the picture of a beautiful ceremony in his church, with Father Joe marrying them. Then they would dance the night away under the star-lit sky. She half-smiled with her swollen lips at the amazing, lovely thought of her and Bryant together forever.

"Ms. Greene, is that a smile I see? Are you enjoying me whipping you? I know you must want more." He hit her hard across her breast, a new and tender place. The sting bit into her skin, and she screamed. Somewhere in the room, she heard them hit Billy again because he still refused to watch Mr. Smith torture her.

Through her swollen lips, she said, "I was thinking about my wedding day with Bryant and how beautiful it will be." She heard his condescending laugh and not even that bothered her anymore.

"Sorry Ms. Greene, but there is no wedding in your future because I plan to use you up until there is nothing left. When your body doesn't fetch me a good price any longer, you will no longer be of any use to me. By then, no one will want you. As I said, there are things worse than death."

Bryant couldn't listen to it anymore—he had to find her. Everyone spread out in the club looking for Macy, but he wanted to be the one to find her. Only he knew how bad her condition was and what was happening to her.

Paul pulled Bryant and his brother through a doorway and down a hall. Once they were inside, they could hear the commotion going on behind one of the doors.

Bryant kicked in the door, and suddenly all hell broke loose. Paul, Mack, Cadman, and Jonathan fought with Mr. Smith's men, while Bryant went to take down Mr. Smith. When Macy tried to open her one good eye, she saw Father Joe taking off his jacket to cover her naked body. He untied her arms, and she fell into his lap. She held on to him for dear life. He whispered in her ear that she was safe now. His hand moved up and down her back as he rocked her gently. Her mind was playing tricks on her, but it felt real.

The rage that came over Bryant was like nothing he had ever felt before. His fist repeatedly hit into the man's face, and the crazed feeling of wanting to kill him was strong. He felt someone pulling him off the man, who now sat in a pool of his own blood.

"Bryant, that's enough you're going to kill him." He realized both Mack and Paul held him back—and just as he felt himself losing control again. The man smiled through the blood and said, "That bitch deserved everything she got." With that, Cadman landed one solid hard punch that knocked the man out flat. Just then, Bobby rushed in with his gun drawn, before recognizing that everything was under control.

Putting away his gun, he said to Bryant, "I thought you were going wait for me." He looked around the room until his eyes landed on Macy.

Bryant thought, Macy—he had to get to Macy. Turning, he found her in the corner in his uncle's arms. He was afraid to go to her, afraid to touch her. Kneeling, he said her name. When she lifted her face to look at him, Bryant's rage returned. The sight of her had Bryant clenching his jaw. He knew he had to tamp it down to take care of her. It wasn't easy, but he didn't want her to see his fury. When Macy said his name, he wanted to wrap her in his arms and never let her go.

The paramedics arrived and started to care for her. They wrapped her in a blanket, but she refused to get onto the stretcher. Once she was in Bryant's arms, she didn't ever want him to let go. The paramedics didn't like Bryant carrying her, but she told them she didn't think she had any broken bones, just cuts, and bruises.

The room cleared out, the paramedics wheeled Billy off, and Bobby cuffed Mr. Smith and handed him to another officer. Just as Bryant started carrying Macy out, she stopped him.

"Wait! I have to tell Bobby something," she said. Bobby stepped up to her. "Bobby, he has the girls. There is a hidden door behind his desk with a button on the wall. The girls are somewhere back there, and all the other clubs are all his too. Please save them."

Bobby said, "You are one amazing woman, Macy Greene." He kissed her forehead because it was the only spot on her face that didn't have cuts and bruises. Bobby turned, talking into his radio, and requesting back up and units to descend on all the other clubs owned by Mr. Smith.

Bryant wanted to get Macy out of there. So far, she hadn't said much, and that scared him. All she kept saying was for him not to let her go, and he had no intention of doing that. Walking out through the club, Macy buried her face in his chest as the paramedics followed. As they cleared the outer door, Bryant saw that his entire family stood on the sidewalk. For once, he loved having a big family.

Raylan had her arm around Tane's waist, and Jonathan stood next to her with his arm on her shoulder. His parents held hands next to Paul, Mack, Patrick, and Gabe. His two sisters huddled together, watching as everyone left the club, either on their own or in handcuffs.

Bryant climbed into the ambulance with Macy. She wouldn't let him put her down, so he sat with her in his lap. Mack appeared in the open doors, "Give me your keys, and I'll get your truck to the hospital." Trying not to jostle Macy as he dug out his keys, he tossed them over to Mack. Macy groaned with his movement, and he knew she had to be in a lot of pain.

As the doors closed, the female paramedic gently started to attend to the gash on Macy's cheek. As she cleaned the cut, the woman looked up at Bryant, and his heart sank from the expression on her face. This was going to be bad. It wasn't just the outward wounds, either. Macy was going to have so much to deal with psychologically. He wanted to press her into him, hugging her hard, but he had to be gentle and hold her away from his body.

Macy sat in Bryant's arms with her eyes closed trying to accept the fact that she was safe. Being in his arms was not a mind game she played with herself to keep going—she was really safe. Bryant had rescued her, and he loved her. She opened her one eye and saw him staring down at her. Knowing how bad she must look, she said, "Don't look at me, I must be a mess."

Bryant whispered, "Are you kidding me? I can't take my eyes off you, in fear you might disappear. The few hours I didn't know where you were, it just about killed me. I will never stop, Macy—looking at you, kissing you, loving you, never." He felt her snuggle in closer to him, and he needed that just as much as she did.

They pulled up to the emergency entrance, and the paramedic said, "Macy, please, we really need you on the stretcher. We don't need Mr. O'Shea falling trying to get out of the ambulance."

Macy nodded her head to show her compliance, but said to Bryant, "Don't let go, okay?"

Bryant felt the knot in his throat as he said, "I have no plans of doing that." He stood and again she groaned as he placed her as gently as he could on the gurney. The blanket slipped away, exposing her leg, and he could see the slashes there as they went across her thigh. Swallowing hard, Bryant covered her again. This was going to kill him, knowing what she went through, and it would take all the strength he had just to get her through this.

They strapped her down, and he held her hand as they moved her into the hospital. Several of his family members were already there, but Bryant didn't acknowledge them, he concentrated only on Macy. He didn't want her to feel embarrassed by the crowd that would no doubt be here soon.

Once they settled her into a room, he took her hand again, pulling the only chair in the small space to her bedside. Placing his forehead on her hand on the side of the bed, he prayed, for her safety, and for the strength to get Macy through this. Feeling her hand slip from his, she reached up and caressed his hair.

Macy whispered, "I'm going to be fine, Bryant. It might take some time, but I will be okay. If you hang in there with me…"

His head popped up so fast it startled her, "No, Macy, there is no if. When you're ready, I plan on giving you that wedding day you thought about."

Macy gasped. "How do you know about that?"

He swallowed hard, "The pen you had in your purse not only records, but it also has a GPS locator, and the capability to transmit what it's recording—as long as you are close. So as soon as I was nearby, I could hear everything the pen picked up."

The shame hit Macy. "So, you know what happened," her voice drifted as she turned her head away from him.

"No Macy, I only heard the end of what he said to you, and believe me, it killed me to have to hear that shit. But it also gave me the smallest bit of comfort, because I knew you were alive."

Macy felt the tears as she said, "I don't want you to know. At least not now."

"Whatever you need Macy, I'm here, today, tomorrow, and forever. Remember, I plan to marry you."

Just then, the curtain drew back. There stood a female doctor. She said, "Knock-knock. Hi, Macy, I'm Doctor Ann, and I'm going to examine you and take care of you." Looking over to Bryant she said, "Do you mind stepping out? The exam won't take long, and then you're welcome to come back."

He looked to Macy, and her grip on his hand tightened. He didn't want to leave her side, but he wondered if he had what it took to stay. He kissed her forehead and said, "I won't go anywhere. I'll be right on the other side of the curtain."

Bryant stepped out and closed his eyes as he heard the Doctor talking to Macy. "Let me see what we have. Did you lose consciousness?"

"No."

"You're going to need stitches for this laceration on your cheek. I'll call for a plastic surgeon." Macy moaned in pain.

"I want to do a full body scan, to make sure you have no internal bleeding. I want to keep you for the night, Macy, to keep an eye on you. It's already late, and by the time, you get all the tests done it will be morning anyway. In the meantime, you will have a room for the night. Macy, now I know this is hard on you, but I have to ask— were you sexually assaulted?"

"No," he heard her say. Bryant finally released the breath he'd been holding.

"He just whipped me with a riding crop as if I was an animal. My arms and shoulders are killing me from hanging so long." She moaned again as if the doctor was examining the area she said hurt.

"Okay, we will have a CAT scan done, and in the meantime, I'll get you some pain meds so you can rest comfortably." The doctor pulled back the curtain and said Bryant could go back in.

They eventually moved Macy to a room upstairs, and with pain medication in her system, she slept. The plastic surgeon came in to stitch her face and several other places. As she slept, they took her for test after test. Bryant waited in her room. He was exhausted but couldn't close his eyes. The things he had heard in the earpiece played in his head like a bad movie.

When they brought Macy back from testing again, this time she was awake, and talking to Bobby Hernandez.

"I found this beautiful lady in the elevator," he said to Bryant. "I was just telling Macy, that she uncovered a huge sex slave ring. I mean, this guy had something going on at each of his clubs. He kept hundreds of people locked up in the basement. He was one sick son of a bitch. Not only did we rescue women, but we found men, little girls, and young boys too. Just sick."

Bryant's jaw dropped.

Bobby continued to say, "Anyway, Macy freed so many people today. So now they can go home to their families. She, cleared a ton of missing person cases today." Bryant knew that what Macy had done was a great thing, but at what cost to her?

Macy's next visitor was from his Uncle Joe. Bryant wasn't surprised to see him. He talked quietly with Macy as Bryant stood back to allow them privacy. He knew his uncle would comfort her. Macy arranged to meet with his uncle again after she got out of the hospital and when her physical wounds healed. As his uncle left Bryant hugged him hard as a silent thank you for taking care of his girl. He was glad when the room was silent again. Macy called him to her bedside, saying, "I need to feel you next to me."

"I don't want to hurt you," Bryant said, but she wouldn't take no for an answer. He was still dirty from working all day, but she didn't care, so he removed his boots and slowly slipped in next to her. She only displayed discomfort until she felt settled in his arms. The sound she made then was one of sheer relief. Bryant found that with her in his arms, he could finally close his eyes. "Macy, do you want me to call your parents?"

She whispered, "I don't want them to know yet. I need a little time." Bryant would do whatever she wanted.

It wasn't long before the nurse came in to take Macy's blood pressure and to make sure she wasn't running a fever. "You know it's against the rules for you to be in her bed," she said. Then she smiled and added, "I'll close the door for you on my way out."

Bryant said, "Macy, when you're released today, please tell me you'll come home with me. I want to take care of you, and I don't think I could stand being apart from you."

"I guess, I didn't even think about it. I just thought that's where I was going because I don't want to be without you. Bryant, I love you, and when things settle down, I want to plan a beautiful wedding."

Bryant smiled so hard his cheeks hurt. "So, I guess we need to do some ring shopping when you feel up to it."

"I want you to pick something out for me, and when the time is right, I want you to ask me, okay?"

He softly touched his lips to hers and said, "I love you too baby, more than you can imagine."

The doctor released Macy midmorning. Bryant was taking her to his house, hopefully, to stay. Walking out of Macy's room, Bryant found his mother and Raylan still in the waiting room. He hadn't even realized they'd been sitting out there the whole time, waiting to hear about Macy's condition. His focus had only been on her. As the nurse pushed Macy's wheelchair, she stopped in front of his family as they approached.

His mother was the first to move to hug Macy. She was very gentle and easy, and she said, "Macy, dear, I'm so glad you're alright. I know that must have been some ordeal for you, but Bryant is going to take good care of you now."

Before his mother could say any more, Bryant told her, "Mom, Macy has agreed to be my wife."

Raylan pumped her fist in the air and yelled, "Whoo-hoo, more girls in the O'Shea family. I knew one day we would overrule the male population."

Bryant saw as a small smile cross Macy's face as she watched his sister's antics. He wasn't sure Macy had wanted to announce it just yet, but with the night they'd had, he felt everyone needed some good news.

Over the next two weeks, Macy's bruises faded, and her stitches came out. She was on the mends physically, but still had a way to go emotionally. Seeing his uncle once or twice a week seemed to help her. Macy still hadn't shared everything that happened to her, but she told him bits and pieces.

Macy's parents came to Bryant's house once she told them what had happened. They weren't happy that she didn't call them right away, but they were glad that Macy was going to be alright. Her parents liked Bryant and went to the O'Shea Sunday dinner. Macy's boss, Mr. Sisco also came to see her and offered Macy, her own column on the newspaper and commended her for a job well done.

Bryant took time off from work to be with Macy. He got her involved in the renovations on the house. They shared ideas and talked about what Macy liked. Bryant drew a design for the banister, and Macy even made a few adjustments. With several projects to work on, Macy's smile and her feisty personality returned. Bryant knew it was time to put that ring on her finger, the one he'd had since the day after she left the hospital.

That evening Bryant lit candles and strung white lights all around out on the front porch in the gazebo area. He set the table with dinner, and then he went to get his future wife. Making Macy close her eyes as he covered them, he led her to his surprise. Once she opened her eyes, her hand went to her mouth.

"Oh Bryant, this is just how I pictured it. It's beautiful." She walked around the intimate space, running her hand over everything.

Bryant had come to know that Macy felt a lot through her hands. When she stopped admiring his work and turned to look at him, he knew he was the luckiest man in the world.

He went down on one knee, Bryant took her hands in his. "Macy, I will love you forever. I promise to cherish you always. I want you to be not only my wife, but also my best friend, my lover, my partner, and the mother of my children. Will you do me the honor of marrying me?"

Macy looked down into the most beautiful blue-green eyes she'd ever see. "Yes," she said without hesitation.

He stood slipping the ring onto her finger. Now she would be his forever.

Epilogue

Raylan O'Shea worked another shift at the pub. Running the kitchen in the family-owned Irish pub was her thing. But lately, it wasn't enough, because she had no personal life. Watching her brother Bryant fall in love with Macy had made Raylan feel her loneliness. Bryant and Macy were planning their wedding in a few months, and Raylan was happy for them—she truly was. After what Macy had gone through, kidnapped by a crazy man, she deserved to be happy.

When Raylan went home smelling like a greasy burger or seared steaks, she didn't feel very attractive. Because of her duties at the pub, she always had her hair tied back in a bandana. Raylan couldn't remember the last time she'd dressed up and gone out to do anything.

Putting all the food away and cleaning the kitchen took from eleven o'clock when the kitchen officially closed for the night until the bar itself closed down. Sometimes, Raylan would use the time to start prepping for the next day, depending on how tired she was.

Most times everyone stayed clear of Raylan's kitchen, but every once in a while, she would have a run-in with one of her brothers or their friends. One in particular usually made a pest out of himself. Her brother Paul's best friend Jonathan Callahan had been flirting with her and chasing after her for years now. She always had a secret crush on him, and if she thought for one minute that he was seriously interested in her, she might have gone after him.

She knew that would never happen because Jonathan never took any woman too seriously. He was only after one thing, and once he got it, he moved on to the next one.

Raylan refused to be one of his many conquests, his piece of ass for the week. She was mumbling to herself when she heard the kitchen door open. Most likely, it was Mack, her older brother. Blocked by the walk-in refrigerator, she couldn't see who it was. When she didn't hear anyone calling her name, she went on with what she'd been doing.

When Raylan turned to leave, the man standing in the doorway startled her. Putting her hand to her heart, she said, "Damn, you scared me. Why didn't you say anything?"

"Because I like watching you," Jonathan said. He stepped into the refrigerator with her.

"I don't have time for your crap tonight. I'm dirty, smelly, and tired."

"Raylan, you know that would never stop me." He moved closer until he had her backed up against the wire racks that lined the walls.

Raylan knew that standing in the walk-in refrigerator, in that tight space with him, wasn't a good idea. She was cold, and she knew that her body would show just how cold, or how hot she was. But Jonathan had his own ideas when he pinned her to the wall.

"Ray, this thing that happened with your brother, you know, with Macy? Well, I can't seem to get it out of my head. When we busted in there, seeing her hanging there covered in blood. God, it makes me mad every time I think about it, and it's never too far from my mind."

"You saw Macy hanging there naked?"

"Yeah, but it's something I wish I hadn't. Don't look at me like that, Ray. There wasn't a thing sexual about it. It was disgusting— she had her own blood covering her body."

"I know the situation is hard for everyone. Macy is doing so much better now though, and Bryant is the happiest I've ever seen him."

"Yeah, and like I said, I've done a lot of thinking, and I'm done chasing you."

Raylan couldn't help the disappointment that rushed through her, and in her defense, she came back with a sassy response, "Time to move on, giving up the good fight, uh."

"It's time for me to catch you," Jonathan said. He kissed her with everything he had, wanting her to know he wasn't playing anymore.

Look for Raylan's story March 2017

Keep reading for a sneak peek of Riptides of Love.

Find me on the web.

Facebook – Trish Collins Author

Instagram – trish_collins_author

Trishcollinsauthor.net

TrishCollins.Author@gmail.com

Amazon.com

CHAPTER ONE

Ben Jacobs was attempting to finish the inventory. He had been working on it all week. Ben despised this part of owning a surf shop, but he knew that if he left it for anyone else, it would be done half-assed. He was the dependable and responsible one. The one that made sure the payroll was in, so everyone got their paychecks. He was the one who kept the store running behind the scenes. Ben was the oldest of three children, and at thirty-five, he took his responsibilities seriously. After his dad's death, Ben and his siblings took over managing the surf shop. Ben had always taken care of his brother and sister as they grew up. If either of them got into trouble, Ben was the one to get them out because he was the one everyone went to when a conflict occurred. He was trustworthy with all of their secrets.

"I have to be the one to make sure we have everything on this list in the store, and it's where it belongs," he said to himself as he moved the merchandise to where it belonged.

Ben thought about how Jeff, his brother and one-third owner of the shop, was out on a date. He always seemed to have a date or something more important to do instead of doing any kind of real work at the shop. Jeff was the partner who made an appearance when he wanted and took off when it suited him. He was irresponsible, easygoing, and didn't take anything too seriously. Jeff never had to because Ben always did. However, Jeff was excellent with the customers and could persuade anyone who came in to look

214

at a surfboard to buy one. He was great with any and all of the females, and when they came in to try on a swimsuit, they wanted to know what he thought. They purchased it if he liked it, and he almost always adored the suit. It was more Jeff and Owen, their younger employee, which moved the merchandise. They just had that cool dude surfer look going for them, and they played the part well. It was something Ben wasn't sure he could pull off anymore, his appearance still that of a surfer, but he thought he was getting a little too old to be acting as if hanging at the beach, and surfing was the most important thing in life.

"I could have asked Mom to help, but then I would have to hear all about how I'm not getting any younger, that I'm not married with a bunch of kids," he said to himself, shaking his head. He knew his mother would lay the guilt trip on him as she always did about how she wanted him married with some grandkids, and since he was the oldest, it was his duty to be first.

Ben hadn't found the right woman, anyone he felt passionate about. His mother made it known that it was one more of his responsibilities, even though all of her children were of age to get married. Ben's mom didn't hold out much hope for Jeff, much less have kids. He never stayed with any girl long enough to learn their names, and as far as Dannie, his sister wasn't ready to make any commitments either. She was younger and having too much fun.

"Are you talking to yourself again?" A voice asked from the front of the store, and Ben looked up from the list in his hand and saw his young employee, Owen Fisher. Ben must have been so deep in thought that he hadn't heard the bell jingle on the door.

"I was just trying to finish up inventory I've been working on all week, and since no one is volunteering to help, I have to have a conversation with myself," talking to Owen over his shoulder. "Are you in here tonight because you have nothing better to do and want to help me, your great employer, on your night off?"

"Well, I would help," Owen moved toward the storage room.

"But?" Ben knew Owen wasn't there to help. He knew he had other plans.

"Yeah, but I have a date," Owen said with a goofy grin.

"Everyone has a date or something else to do that's more important," Ben needed to get a life.

"I have some time before I have to pick her up, so I can help." Ben wouldn't make Owen stay.

"Nah, that's okay. I'm almost done anyway, so what did you need?" Owen blushed as he looked away from Ben. "So," Ben wasn't sure what Owen wanted from the back storage room.

"So, I came in to get stuff from the back, the blanket, and the basket." Owen wanted to grab the stuff and go before Ben talked to him about being responsible and mature.

"Oh, I see, so you're going down to the beach," Ben was observing Owen's behavior, examining him a little closer now.

Owen's face got a little red, and Ben knew what that meant. It was code for sex on the beach. Ben looked Owen in the eye and said, "You have what you need to protect yourself, right?"

Owen didn't want to have this talk with Ben now, but he knew he was only looking out for him, so he said, "Yeah, I have everything I need, although not sure if I'll need it, but yeah, sure, I got it."

"Okay, then go have fun on your date, and don't get caught." Ben smiled at Owen.

"You know it. Hey, when's the last time you had a date?" Owen asked since Ben was no longer scrutinizing him.

"I have better things to do with my time," Ben laughed.

"Yeah, like what, inventory?" Owen shook his head at Ben as he went to get the basket and blanket out of the back room.

"I haven't found anybody that I want to take out on a date, okay," Ben said as he thought of how nice it would be to have someone and knew as the words came out of his mouth that it was lame but true. Even though many were interested, there hadn't been a woman to pique his interest in a very long time. Owning a surf shop attracted many it was one of the benefits, but he couldn't just take what they offered freely, not as Jeff did. That wasn't Ben's style because he needed more.

Maybe he was getting too mature and responsible for his own good. Ben was just considering how he needed to get out more when Owen pulled him out of his pity party.

"I know someone you can ask out. She's new in town," Owen said with a big smirk.

"Oh yeah, I'm not sure you're the one to pick a woman for me." Ben wasn't sure if he could choose someone either. "She'd have to be older than twenty-five," he said with a laugh.

"Oh, she is older, well not that old, you know, like your age, maybe younger. She came in earlier today when you were in your office. Her name is Liz. She wanted some surfing info. I think she said she's writing a book or something like that."

"And why should I consider asking her out?" Ben wasn't sure he wanted to know.

"Because she's hot. You do remember what a hot chick looks like, right?" That got Ben's attention.

"Oh, aren't you hilarious, and how would you know what is hot on an older chick?" Owen just smiled at Ben.

"Hey, just because she is too old for me doesn't mean I can't see what's in front of me."

Ben thought that maybe he should find out a little more about this older, hot-as-hell chick. "Okay, I'll bite. What does she look like?" Ben wondered just how old this older woman was.

Owen gave it some thought, and after a minute or two, he said, "She has fiery red wavy hair that goes to her shoulders and the greenest eyes you've ever seen. Her body is to die for, and even I could see how hot she was, big boobs, a small waist, and a sweet ass."

"Well, you seemed to get a really good look at all her assets. Did you get her age?" Ben shook his head, "So glad we pay you to keep extremely good track of all the customers." Ben was intrigued by the description of the woman. A redhead, the thought was appealing.

"Well, the hot ones, anyway. I always keep my eyes open," Owen was starting to walk away.

Ben started laughing and wanted to change the subject, "Hey, are you still going to be able to surf in the morning after your exhausting date tonight? The waves are going to be big, so I hear. I'm not sure if Jeff is going to grace us with his presence. I'm sure it'll depend on how late of a night he has. You know we'll hear all about it because he'll have no problem rubbing it in," Owen stopped walking and turned toward Ben.

"I'm not planning to be out that late. I'll be there at the crack of dawn," Owen said as he made a face at Ben. "I'm not old like you and Jeff. I can stay up all night and still be out there surfing for hours and blow you two away."

"You really do think you're a comedian? Hey, don't quit your day job. Oh yeah, you work for me." Ben called as Owen started to head for the door again.

"Maybe you need to go on that date with the redhead, then you can brag about how late your night was and give Jeff a run for his money," Owen said as he looked back at Ben.

Ben wasn't sure he could ever give Jeff any real competition because Jeff loved all females. Ben wanted to experience something with the person he was spending time with because, for him, it was quality, not quantity. However, quality hadn't come so easy for Ben, not lately, anyway. When he was younger, he thought he would end up married to Jenny, his high school sweetheart, and they would start a family together. However, she went off to college, met someone else, and wanted a career, not a surf shop in California. Ben and his brother Jeff had to stay behind to run the shop instead of going to college. Dannie didn't hang around for long after she got out of college, either. She wanted a life that didn't have anything to do with surfing, and now it was just Jeff, their mom, and him. Mom helped with the books and some of the office work, but most of the time, she was there to keep track of her boys and interfere in their lives. She wanted to make sure that she was right in the center of their lives.

"So, hello, are you going to ask her out or not? If you want some help, I can help you with some lines guaranteed to get you some action." Owen had a half smile on his face, knowing Ben's reaction.

"I don't know, maybe if she comes back in and is as hot as you say. I just might, you never know." Ben didn't want to give Owen the satisfaction of knowing he was interested.

"Ok, if you say so, because I just happen to know she's coming tomorrow afternoon because I'm going to teach her all about the surfboards. I guess you can kinda say I already have a date with her." Owen paused, then added, "Unless you want to do it."

"I think you need to get going on that date you have, and I need to finish up here so I can get some sleep if I'm going to keep up with you tomorrow," Ben blew out a breath.

When Ben woke the next morning, thoughts of getting to the beach to do some surfing came to mind. He wondered what the day ahead would bring. Would the waves be as challenging as the weather conditions were hinting, they might be? As Ben got his coffee going, he sat at the breakfast bar in his kitchen and started to think about what Owen had said about the redhead. He thought of all the women he'd socialized with in the last couple of years. He knew that none of them suited him, not that he had a commitment problem. The precise one just hadn't come along, at least, that's what he'd been telling himself.

Ben half put on his wetsuit, got his board, and set out for the beach. When he got to the spot where they enjoyed surfing, he found Owen waiting for him. Ben knew he was in for it because Owen would give him shit for being late. The kid seemed to have more energy than anyone he knew. Oh, to be young again, he thought as he leisurely walked toward him.

Owen was sitting on the beach, looking out at the waves. "It's about damn time you got here. I've been waiting thirty minutes for you."

"Yeah, yeah, so I'm old and slow. Give me a break," Ben blew out a breath.

Owen laughed and said, "Well, at least you know it, but I'm not giving you any breaks."

"Thanks, you're such a great kid, so remind me to dock your pay this week," Ben said jokingly. Now Ben was smiling as Owen stuck his tongue out at him.

"What, are you two now?" Ben grinned at Owen.

Ben sat beside Owen and asked, "How was your date?"

"It was ok." Owen looked out over the water even though it was still dark.

"Just ok, what? No bragging, not even about how late you were out?"

"I don't kiss and tell, you're going to have to get your own girl, or you can hear all about Jeff's social life if he shows up," Owen turned to look at Ben.

"Since when, you always have something to boast about? You're Jeff's best competition. I think sometimes he is a bad influence on you." Ben could see so much of Jeff in Owens's intentions toward his girlfriends.

"What am I responsible for now?" a voice came from behind as Jeff walked up.

"You're being a bad influence on Owen." Ben stood, pulled his wetsuit the rest of the way up, and grabbed his board.

"Hey, it's not my fault if he is a fast learner and that you have no knowledge to share with him on the subject. It's not like he's going around breaking hearts all over town. He's a decent kid."

"I didn't say he wasn't a great kid. He just has a different girl all the time, like someone else I know."

"Okay, just because you're not getting any doesn't mean the rest of us have to suffer. I, on the other hand, had a great time last night," Jeff said with a big lopsided smile.

"Hey, are you girls going to surf, or are you going to argue all day? The waves are waiting." As Owen got up and ran for the water, he called over his shoulder, "Are you coming, or are you too old and feeble?"

That got both Ben and Jeff's attention, "I think we should drown him and say a shark got him or cut his ripcord and make him have to swim in," Jeff said.

"Yeah, or we can make him work the next four weekends in a row," Ben replied.

"Boy, hit him where it hurts. Remind me not to piss you off," Jeff said as they paddled out.

The sun was coming up, and it was a beautiful sunrise. It was supposed to be a gorgeous day, and the waves were great. What more could anyone want? Ben thought while sitting on his board, waiting for the next wave, and contemplating the redhead, yet again. If she was as hot as Owen said, maybe he might actually get laid and break his very long dry spell. He knew he couldn't have meaningless sex because he wasn't about putting his dick in someone that was just a body and no soul. He was pulled from his thoughts when Jeff paddled by and caught a wave to the shore.

"I'm here to surf, not to feel sorry for myself. I just need to get it together," he said to himself.

"Talking to yourself again; maybe you are getting old. Thirty-five, and you're starting to lose it." Ben hadn't realized that Owen had paddled up next to him. "I thought you were here to surf, clear your mind, and enjoy the waves," Owen said.

"Yeah, I am. I'll get the next one," Ben paddled hard to catch the next wave.

Owen laughed, shook his head, as he said, "I don't want to end up like him talking to myself."

Ben caught the next few big waves, challenging Mother Nature and trying not to consider his life or the lack of one. After a couple good hours of surfing, things would look better, it always did. It was relaxing and mind-cleansing. It was just what Ben needed to get away from everything.

Ben listened as Owen expressed to Jeff how his ride was exceptionally better, and his skill surpassed and was superior to Jeff's. The way the banter flew back and forth, you would think the three of them were brothers. Owen was like a little brother in so many ways. He had been working for them for so long and was a part of the family. Ben could remember when Owen had gone through the surfing clinic when he was just thirteen. He was such a natural and got bit by the surfing bug. Owen started hanging around the shop and asking questions, and before they knew it, he was very knowledgeable with the surfboards. He was almost as knowledgeable as Jeff was.

When Owen was fifteen, he asked if he could work at the shop, and since he was already selling boards by talking with whoever would listen to him, it was a no brainer, and work kept him out of trouble. His home life wasn't the best, only having his mother. Before he started surfing and hanging around the shop, his mom had said he was a handful, but Owen had come a long way. He was going to community college in the fall, and Ben felt pride to know that they had some influence over how Owen conducted himself.

He was very proud of Owen because he really was turning into a very outstanding young adult. Ben thought about how he would do just about anything for him, even paying Owen's college tuition. He wanted him to have something he didn't get to have.

~ ~ ~ ~ ~ ~

Liz McGreary lay in the largest bed she had ever seen. The bed was one of those big four-poster beds with sheer white curtains that went all the way to the floor. It was four A.M., and she looked up at the vaulted ceiling, wondering what she was doing there. As a romance writer, she never got much sleep, as it was always when she started to write a new book, all those ideas running around in her head. However, this time it wasn't just the new book to keep her from her restful slumber. Just the fact that she was here all alone and her daughter Paige was on the other side of the country. She hadn't expected to feel so alone in this huge house, but she was used to always having Paige with her because it had been just the two of them for so long.

When Paige went into third grade, Liz started home-schooling her so that when she had to go out of town for book signings or go to meetings with her agent, she would just bring Paige with her. Paige would go off with friends and sometimes spend the night away. She even went on a few vacations with friends, but this was not the same empty feeling. Somehow, it felt so much more permanent. Liz knew she would have to deal with the loneliness, but she hadn't expected that it would feel similar to how she felt when her husband Michael died ten years ago. The loneliness was overwhelming. She told herself Paige was alive, just not with her every day.

Paige wasn't gone for good, but she had grown up and was starting her own life, and all Liz had to do was pick up the phone to talk to her. Liz overcame the emotional distress of her husband's death because she had to because she had to take care of her daughter. Paige became Liz's whole life, and everything revolved around what Paige wanted and needed.

Liz's daughter was going to come with her, spending the last summer with her before heading off to college in August, but Paige got an exceptionally good offer for an internship. This internship could land her a great job after graduation. So, as much as Liz wanted to try to accept the fact that Paige was growing up and had turned eighteen, Liz couldn't help feeling very alone. She knew she would have to overcome the empty nest feelings that would come when Paige left for school, but she didn't think she'd be working through them so soon. She thought she'd have this month with her in California, having fun on the beach while she did research for the new book.

Liz knew she wouldn't get any more sleep, so she threw off the covers and headed to the kitchen to start a pot of coffee. As the smell filtered through the air, the cobwebs from lack of sleep in Liz's head cleared. She sat on one of the brass bar stools at the breakfast nook, grabbed her pad from her purse, and started to write down some of the questions she wanted to ask the kid from the surf shop today. She needed to get her mind back on work and off missing Paige. She needed to learn all that she could while she was here. She had an appointment this afternoon to learn about the surfboards with the young man she had met yesterday. Liz thought about how cute the young man was and how Paige would be sorry that she didn't come after all. Owen was what he said his name was, and he seemed very nice and helpful.

"Well, I will just have to send a picture to Paige of Owen to rub it in," she said to herself.

After completing her list of questions for Owen and while finishing her first cup of coffee, Liz contemplated what she would do with her life and all her free time, time that she had always devoted to Paige. What was in the future for her now that her daughter was growing up and wouldn't need her so much anymore? After Michael's death, Liz had to be the breadwinner. She was a stay-at-home mom at the time and needed to figure out how to support herself and a child. Michael had a sizable life insurance policy, but Liz knew it wouldn't last forever. She had gone to night classes at the community college and got her English degree. Liz had always loved to write, so she tried writing while she was at home taking care of her daughter. As it turned out, she had done very well, and it worked out for both of them. Liz worked from home and was there for Paige. It was a struggle, in the beginning, to get her first books published, but once she found a good agent, things went well.

"Well, I made a life for myself before, and I guess I have no other choice. I'll have to do it again." Liz said to herself. She got up to pour herself another cup of coffee. "I need to take my coffee out to that huge deck and enjoy the sunrise."

Liz went through the large French doors to sit on one of the big lounge chairs with the cushions that were so soft and thick. She wrapped herself up in the blanket that was sitting on the back of the chair. It was chilly this time of morning. It was still a little dark, but the sun would be up soon. Liz could hear the waves crashing on the beach and smelled the salt in the air.

"Man, the waves sound so rough out there, but the air is so clean and refreshing," Liz said to herself as she took a big breath of the salty air and tried to relax.

"I have to stop talking to myself, or someone will think I'm going crazy. I'll be that lonely old lady all the kids talk about." Liz laughed at herself and closed her eyes to enjoy the sounds of being at the beach. As she lay there, she could hear people talking and laughing. Liz got up to check to see if it was people walking or running on the beach. She looked over the railing of the deck and squinted to see. She could barely see them, but there were surfers out there. *Oh, God, no way, there are people out there in the water. You could barely see.* "Are they crazy?"

Liz threw off the blanket and went back inside to her bedroom to change out of her nightshirt and shorts, grabbing a pair of jeans and a big sweatshirt. Liz pulled her top and jeans on as fast as she could and ran into the bathroom, washed her face, pulled her hair into a ponytail, and brushed her teeth. She went back into the kitchen to grab her notebook with her questions on it and her cell phone as she was heading out the door. If the crazy surfers don't kill themselves, then she wouldn't have to call 911. She could always try to ask them some questions.

Liz walked down the old, weathered staircase that led to the beach. As the sun was coming up, she could see that there were three guys out there. She walked to the part of the beach where the surfers were and sat down, getting comfortable. She watched everything they were doing out there with wonder and appreciation. It surprised her their commitment to capturing the massive waves. The turbulence of Mother Nature filled her with anxiety and anticipation, and she wondered whether they'd stay on top of their boards. At times, it was beautiful and physically passionate the way their muscles moved. Some rides were disappointing, but she found their single-minded determination impressive. It was unbelievably entertaining to see the skill they mastered, but at the same time, she was very aware of the danger. She could hear them yelling to each other after one had ridden a wave. They looked like they were having so much fun out there. But it still was crazy to want to stand on a board that you had to fight to stay on just for the thrill of it.

"I can't see how risking my life to stand on a board and ride a wave is worth it, as much as it may be fun, and the waves are so enormous that it just wouldn't be amusing to me, it would be insane.

227

It wouldn't be worth my life. It must be the mother in me," she said quietly to herself.

Liz watched them take wave after wave, and it was cool to watch how they moved their body this way and that to stay on the board. There were a few bad wipe outs that made her grab her phone and hold her breath until a head popped back out of the water. They laughed at each other and yelled out how cool they thought the ride was. As Liz watched, she could see they were wearing wetsuits.

"I guess the water is cold this time of the morning. I wonder what they wear under their wetsuits."

That got Liz thinking oh yeah, what would it be like to watch them come out of the water and strip the wetsuit off right in front of her? The thought got Liz all hot, and she realized it could be a scene in her book, so she pulled her pad out and wrote it down. He would be tall and have broad shoulders with bulging muscles. Liz was writing on her pad exactly how she saw her surfer. He'd have long dark wavy hair, almost untamed looking, with dark eyes and a defined jaw line. Yeah, he was sounding good, really good. Liz could feel the tingle start down in between her legs.

"Okay, stop that, no one is going to come out of the water and strip for you. What are you thinking?" She laughed at herself when someone calling her name pulled her out of her fantasy. She looked up to see one of the surfers coming out of the water and heading her way. "Who can that be? I don't know anyone here," she said.

As the surfer got closer, she recognized the blonde young man who was coming up the beach. "Hey Liz, I thought that was you," Owen was smiling at her.

"Oh, Owen, I didn't know that was you out there. Are you crazy?"

Owen started to laugh, "Why do you say that?"

"Oh, I don't know, maybe because it looked like you were going to get killed out there. I had my phone ready a couple of times just in case I had to dial 911," Liz looked like a concerned mother.

"Are you staying around here?" Owen was looking over his shoulder at the other surfers. As she was talking to Owen, the other two guys were starting to come out of the water, and Owen waved to them to come over.

"Yeah, I'm staying right there," as Liz pointed to the house she was renting. "Are they your friends?" nodding her head in the direction of the other guys.

"Well, sort of, yeah, they are friends, but mostly they are my bosses they own the surf shop."

"Oh, okay"

"Hey Ben, come here. I want you to meet someone," Owen yelled over his shoulder.

As Liz watched two very large men walk over to them, she thought to herself oh God, here were two very big, tall, and hot guys standing in front of her.

"Ben, this is the lady I was telling you about last night, the one that is writing the book and wants my help," Owen grinned at Ben.

Ben's eyes stared down at her, and she couldn't help feeling very small. As she looked up at the two men, all she could think of was how strong and muscular they looked in their wetsuits. The thought of her surfer for the book came to life right before her eyes.

"Ben, Jeff, this is Liz. She's here doing research on surfing."

Liz stood wiping her butt, and she still didn't come up to their shoulders. She reached out to shake Jeff's hand and couldn't help but notice his golden-brown eyes and a great smile. Liz thought I bet that the girls just love him. He had light brown hair that was a little shaggy with that sun-kissed look to it from being outside.

"Nice to meet you," Liz noticed Jeff's hand was cold from the water.

When Liz turned to face Ben, she got this funny sensation inside. Here was the surfer she just described in her note pad. When she looked up into Ben's eyes, his very dark eyes, and reached out to shake his hand, something happened to her because she couldn't speak. A shock ran up her arm when his huge hand touched hers. She pulled back fast as if he had burned her. Liz's eyes widened as she stared at her hand. She was trying to figure out what just happened to her. She has never had that reaction to anyone before.

Oh my God, I need to breathe because I don't want to look as if I'm a high school girl trying to talk to the best-looking boy in school. Yet she knew that's exactly how she looked, that deer caught in the headlights look. Ben looked at her with his deep dark chocolate brown eyes, oh, and his dark hair.

"So," Ben said because she didn't say anything. "I hear you're coming in this afternoon to pick Owen's little brain, and I sense that shouldn't take too long. Maybe I could take you for lunch and show you around a bit." Ben couldn't help himself. He had to get to know her. As he looked deep into the most beautiful green eyes he had ever seen, he knew he had to touch her again. Would he feel that surge? He could feel the lust, undeniable chemistry between them.

"Oh, okay," Liz said so quietly. Ben almost missed it.

Liz was thinking, I'm a well-educated woman and a writer, and the best I could come up with was, "Oh okay," how weak. I have a bigger vocabulary than that. I could have said I'd love to, or that would really be nice. After a long-unspoken moment, the uncomfortableness stretched out.

Jeff looked at Liz and then to his brother. They were both staring at each other. "Well, we have to get back to open the store soon, it was nice to meet you, Liz, and when you get bored with my brother, you can come see me, and I'll show you the happening nightlife," Jeff said with one of those killer smiles.

Liz looked away from Ben to see Jeff's smile, the one she was sure he gave all the girls. Ben gave Jeff a big shove that almost knocked him off his feet. Then when Jeff recovered, he went after Ben. They started wrestling right there on the beach. Liz looked on, stunned at what was taking place. They looked more like two boys having a playground fight rather than two very large grown men.

Liz must have been frowning because when Owen looked at her, he said, "Oh, don't mind them. They're just idiots. I think maybe you should just skip going out with either one of them and stay with the mature one, and that would be me," Owen smiled.

As Liz looked at Owen, she could see he was learning some of those lady killer tricks. Oh, how that great smile could melt a young girl's heart. Maybe it was a good thing Paige hadn't come. Liz could see how Paige would fall hard for Owen because how could any girl not. He was tall and tan with his long wavy blonde hair and a nice young man's body.

Owen yelled, "Okay girls, we have to go to work. We have a surf shop to open." That pulled Liz out of her thoughts about Owen and Paige. She looked back toward Ben as they grabbed their surfboards and started to walk away. Ben turned as if he knew she was watching him and said, "See you later, Liz."

"Didn't I tell you she was hot?" Owen punched Ben in the arm.

As they left, Liz could hear Ben tell Jeff there was no way in hell he would let his brother date her. Liz stood there for a few minutes to get her bearings. She thought about how Ben's touch affected her. She had never felt anything like it, not even with her husband, and she wasn't sure what to make of it. Liz could feel the sensation of her breasts tightening, and her whole body was tingling on alert. Ben's sensual mouth tempted her with his grin. He had a toe-curling, totally hot body that her best fantasies couldn't match. The arousal hammered through her veins. How would it feel to have him hold and kiss her? All this anticipation and lust-induced excitement was overpowering her. She looked out over the water to try to breathe and calm her emotions.

"I just need to get back to work on my book, I can use all this sexual frustration for my characters, and it will make the erotic relationship between them more real. It's great when you're the one controlling fate when it's all fiction."

Liz decided to take a walk on the beach. There were no other people walking. She could use the exercise and the fresh air. The water was cold, so she walked where the waves had made the sand hard but not where it could get her wet. Liz thought it would be nice to walk every morning. Did Ben surf every morning? She started to consider what could be happening to her with Ben. She was going to have lunch with him but wasn't sure how she would pull that one off, considering she couldn't even come up with a few words to say on the beach with other people around. She just stood there staring at him. What was she going to do when they were alone? Liz didn't have the smooth moves or the wit when it came to men, and when the man looked like Ben, there was no telling what would happen.

Liz decided to head back to the house because a nice hot shower sounded good. She was getting cold, and she hadn't realized it because she was so overheated trying to talk to Ben. How could she feel so hot on the inside yet be cold? Her fingers felt like ice, "Just what the hell is wrong with me? I don't have trouble talking to men, and I don't get all hot and bothered over them, either. But Ben, I just don't know what I'm doing or how to act around him."

Liz tried breathing, but she had to stop walking as she bent over, putting her hands on her knees, attempting to catch her breath while trying to avoid having an anxiety attack. The stress was getting to her; it must have something to do with Paige going off to college and the lack of sleep. Liz had forgotten all about the situation with Paige for a moment. Wow, she didn't think anything could make her forget that.

Made in the USA
Columbia, SC
04 July 2023

19908800R00134